AMANDA CROSS
THE COLLECTED STORIES

In the Last Analysis
The James Joyce Murders
Poetic Justice
The Theban Mysteries
The Question of Max
Death in a Tenured Position
Sweet Death, Kind Death
No Word from Winifred
A Trap for Fools
The Players Come Again
An Imperfect Spy

AMANDA CROSS

THE COLLECTED STORIES

BALLANTINE BOOKS • NEW YORK

All rights reserved under International and Pan-American
Copyright Conventions. Published in the United States by
Ballantine Books, a division of Random House, Inc., New York,
and simultaneously in Canada by
Random House of Canada Limited, Toronto.

The stories in this work were originally published in *Ellery
Queen's Mystery Magazine* and in the following books: *Malice
Domestic 2* (Pocket Books), *Reader, I Murdered Him* (The
Women's Press), *Reader, I Murdered Him, Too* (The Women's
Press), *A Woman's Eye* (Delacorte), *A Woman's Eye: A Second
Glance* (Delacorte).

http://www.randomhouse.com

Library of Congress Cataloging-in-Publication Data
Cross, Amanda, 1926–
[Short stories. Selections]
The collected stories of Amanda Cross.
p.   cm.
Contents: Tania's nowhere–Once upon a time–Arrie and Jasper–
The disappearance of Great Aunt Flavia–Murder without a text–
Who shot Mrs. Byron Boyd?–The proposition–The George Eliot
play–The baroness.
ISBN 0-345-40817-9
1. Detective and mystery stories, American. 2. Fansler, Kate
(Fictitious character)–Fiction. 3. Women detectives–United
States–Fiction. I. Title.
PS3558.E4526A6   1997
813'.54–dc20   96-42006
CIP

Manufactured in the United States of America
First Edition: January 1997
10 9 8 7 6 5 4 3 2 1

CONTENTS

꙰

INTRODUCTION

⟨∾∾⟩

In 1987, I had faithfully prom-
ised the publisher of a Carolyn Heilbrun book that I would
not work on another Kate Fansler novel until I had finished the nonfiction work then edging toward completion.
The promise was made in all sincerity, but Kate Fansler,
who rather resented being ignored for too long, was
putting up a certain amount of fuss. I had not published a
novel about her since 1986, and that one was written
before 1985; she was growing restless. To those who have
never created a series detective this may sound a bit mad;
to those who have, however, it will hardly raise an eyebrow. Simenon reported how Maigret would intercept him
if too long ignored; likewise Kate Fansler, who is inclined
to hover when disregarded. Still, I had promised not to
work on a novel.

It was then that the thought of a story about Kate Fansler
came to me. I had, in fact, before the prohibition, been
wondering intermittently if I might not use Fansler's niece,

Leighton Fansler (introduced in *Death in a Tenured Position*), as a sort of Watson—an idea that occurred to Leighton herself. And the next thing I knew, Leighton was reporting on Kate Fansler's search for Tania. Once started, I wrote two more stories in this mode after "Tania's Nowhere": "Once Upon a Time" and "Arrie and Jasper," and all were sold to *Ellery Queen's Mystery Magazine*. By this time my Carolyn Heilbrun manuscript—it was *Writing a Woman's Life*—had been completed and I was again able to contemplate my detective in a book-length adventure.

The next four stories and the last story, "The Baroness," were each written in later years at the request of someone who was editing an anthology. In only one of them, "The Disappearance of Great Aunt Flavia," does Leighton Fansler serve as narrator. "The George Eliot Play" is, however, the only story included here that has not previously been published; it was written especially for this collection and is entirely accurate in all its George Eliot facts.

The last story in this collection, "The Baroness," is not a Kate Fansler story. This in no way indicates an intention to desert her or, worse, to allow her to desert me. It happened that at the moment when Sara Paretsky asked for a story to go into her second collection of the adventures of women private eyes and amateur detectives, I was intrigued with the idea of the relationship between two Englishwomen who had been friends from girlhood, but one of whom had moved, upon marriage, to America. I therefore used the American friend as the narrator in the only first-person story or novel I have ever written.

I am not a particular devotee of the detective short story, much preferring novel-length mysteries. I have noticed that I tend to read stories when an author's longer works have captured my attention, when I find I like a certain author's style of writing, and, most compellingly, when my interest in her or his detective urges me to search out more adventures in that fictional life. Thus, for example, I have read Dorothy Sayers's short stories about Peter Wimsey, and even those about her wine salesman, Montague Egg, but her stories without either detective appeal less to me. I mention this predilection of mine to explain why I thought these stories might be of interest to some readers who had found themselves attracted to Kate Fansler and the life she leads and has led.

Something else about them occurred to me as I read over these stories. They suggest that Kate has dabbled—a verb she would resent—in more cases than the novels comprehend. In all of them, however, she is absolutely the amateur, not only without pay and without any of the clout of a professional detective, but also involved only in cases where her sympathies, her knowledge of literature and the academic world, and her sense of rightness are caught. In each case, it is highly unlikely that anyone else would have been in a position to work on the puzzles, or to have been called upon by those in need of Kate's ministrations. She is, in each case, the only one who could, without question, understand what the "fuss" was all about. This is also true, of course, of the American woman in the "The Baroness."

I have always been unsettled by the television stories about Jessica Fletcher, played by Angela Lansbury. The character and the actress are both appealing, but the fact that everywhere Fletcher goes someone is brutally murdered does give one pause—at least it does me. Private eyes, policepersons, and other detectives are called upon when their singular talents are needed. Jessica Fletcher, on the contrary, seems not only to invite the murders she solves, but to engage with murders in unimaginably different settings. Why anyone ever allows her to visit is the deepest mystery of all.

Although Kate Fansler, like Jessica Fletcher, is an amateur, helping those who know her and who realize that her special talents and training can serve them, she does not live amid multiple murders. Indeed, she has been criticized, not always kindly, for not tripping over enough bodies. There are fewer bodies than there are novels, if truth be told.

In only two of these stories is there a body: I am more interested in what I guess can be defined and condemned as intellectual mysteries, that is, stories where one mind must outwit or outguess another. There is a chance for the reader, like Kate, if not to unravel one of life's minor mysteries, at least to recognize the rich variety of human motives. Neither Kate nor I believe that any human condition, individual or collective, is rectified easily or by drastic action. Revolution, revenge, and self-protectiveness almost always outrun the intentions of their instigators. Kate Fansler's way is to aid justice where she can, and if she is involved in the punishment of a criminal, it is only because he has been tempted to betray himself. When Kate is finished with a case, a small degree of order has been restored, a few people are happier, or at least more knowledgeable, but no institution has been profoundly changed.

Kate has never fired a gun or been beaten up in the course of her work, although, like any city dweller, she might be shot or beaten up in the streets any day now. Within the narratives that compose her life, she likes conversation, courtesy, and knowledge. She is drawn to those for whom hatred or reform of others is not a goal. Mysteries intrigue her, arrogance depresses her, and she enjoys a drink rather oftener than a doctor might recommend. She is given to occasional bouts of acedia, a sin not encountered in the Ten Commandments; the purpose of life now and then evades her grasp. She finds some men more attractive than is altogether comfortable in the light of her happy marriage.

As her creator, I cannot claim to be like Kate in any particular respect, but she does represent a commitment to truth and friendship—and a kind of crazy courage—that I admire but can only aspire to. She is richer than I am, thinner, braver, and a more devoted drinker. As with all fictional detectives, she represents a fantasy, but, I hope, not a malignant or violent one. My major wish for her is that some people might enjoy her company and seek it out.

—AMANDA CROSS

Tania's Nowhere

My name is Leighton Fans-
ler. I have long wanted to publish some of the cases of
my aunt, Kate Fansler, who, while never a private investigator in any professional sense—she certainly never had a
license nor was she paid—took on, like Sherlock Holmes
and Peter Wimsey, many interesting cases. She has been
adamant until now about her refusal to let me tell the stories of any of her cases, and no one can be more adamant
than Kate Fansler. I finally got her to admit, however, that
this case was an exception. All those intimately concerned
with it are now dead, and no harm could be done to
anyone in the telling of it. Indeed, she mused, it might be
of help to some.

WHAT WAS CLEAR to Kate at the very beginning of the case
was that, by the time Tania Finship was sixty-two and
almost the oldest member of the faculty in her department,

or anywhere else, she had become beloved. After her disappearance, it became clear that, in the opinion of her colleagues and students, she had not known this. She had done her job efficiently, curtly, honorably, and without notable tact, and had undoubtedly considered, if she reflected on the matter at all, that the outrage and anger she heard from students who had not done well in her courses represented the general opinion. As is, alas, so often the case among human beings—who tend, whatever their profession, to substitute tardy regret for timely expressions of appreciation—Tania Finship was gone before anyone had told her that they loved her.

If she was dead, there was no evidence to say so. Had her husband wished to claim her savings and remarry, he would have been hard put to do so before the statutory seven years. As it was, he mourned her, having always loved her and made his affection clear, if unspoken. She may have kept her professorship through tenure, as many disgruntled younger professors had been heard to mutter, but she kept her marriage because it suited them both: in the United States in those years one did not stay married unless one chose. Her children, grown and moved away, had come east when she disappeared, and finally returned to the West Coast, keeping in close touch with their father. As to her savings, all she and Tom, her husband, owned they had owned jointly. It was already his, but, as he often made clear after the disappearance, sharing it once again with her was his only, his fervent wish.

No one could imagine what had become of her. The police were as puzzled as the FBI and the CIA, who had entered the case on the thinnest of suspicions that she had been part of a spy ring. Her parents had been Marxists and Trotskyites in the Twenties and Thirties, and one never knew for sure that they had not become Stalinists and planted Tania for future spying at birth. Unlikely, but the CIA is nothing if not expert at the unlikely. She might have waited all those years, until her children were grown, and then taken off with her ill-gotten information. What information a professor of Russian literature could have acquired in a blameless life was at best unclear, at worst nonsense. Still, she did read and speak Russian, and what is more, had been clearly heard to say critical things about the United States Government. Anything might be suspected of someone as profoundly antinuclear and antiwar as Tania.

"Which," as Fred Monson said to Kate Fansler, "is just the problem. The CIA has got this ridiculous bee in their bonnet, but the result is everyone has just decided she's in Russia and stopped looking—everyone who had the ghost of a chance of finding her, that is. And the students are getting restless. They've heard her hold forth, and they're perfectly sure leaving this country or even her penthouse for more than a few hours was the last thing she wanted. If Tania had ever had any wanderlust, she had long since lost it, or so the students and her husband reported. The point is, can you help us? I've heard a lot about you."

"What do you think happened?" Kate Fansler asked.

Fred Monson heaved a great sigh. "I try not to think," he said. "The fact is, Tania was a bit of a burden in the department. Conscientious, heavens yes, and hardworking, and highly intelligent. But she had taken to cultivating a crusty manner that was as hard on her colleagues as it was on her students. You want an example? All right: at a meeting of the curriculum committee some weeks ago, when we were discussing next year's catalog, I had to report that some man who had promised to teach the survey course was now refusing to do so. Tania was in charge of survey courses, and was considerably annoyed, as anyone would be at that news that late. What she said was: 'Couldn't we just tell him to go pee up a rope?' "

"I see what you mean," Kate said. "You're not suggesting that the man in question heard about it and abducted her?"

"I'm not suggesting anything—certainly not that. But it's hard enough to run a language department. They're the worst kind: for some reason those who teach languages become ornery from the moment they learn about inflected nouns, without having them talk nothing but mayhem, kidnapping, and worse. Find out what happened to her, please, for the sake of the academic world and my sanity. The department has discretionary funds, and the university will help, all on the q.t., of course. The university position is that she needed an emergency operation, and doesn't want anyone to know. They may have to admit a scandal, but not before it's absolutely necessary."

"I should think," Kate Fansler said, "that the feelings of the university were not anyone's prime concern. They certainly wouldn't be mine. You've checked the hospitals?"

"Everything has been checked," Fred Monson said. "Everything. When my mother used to lose things, she always said they had disappeared into thin air. Of course, they always turned up fifteen minutes later. If there's one thing I can't stand, it's clichés enacting themselves. Tania's nowhere, Goddamn it. Nowhere."

"I'll think about it," Kate Fansler said. "I'll let you know my decision in a few days. Meanwhile, may I talk to Tania's husband? Will he see me?"

"I'll damn well make sure he'll see you," Fred Monson said. Kate could not but reflect that, chancy as the Chair's disposition clearly was, this disappearance had done nothing to improve it. Could Tania have simply decided to vanish for the sheer joy of ruining Fred Monson's life and temper? Or could the husband, however devoted he was reported to be, also have inspired such retribution?

One hour with Tom Finship proved that speculation as unsubstantial as all the others had been. He greeted Kate in the penthouse on Riverside Drive he had long shared with his vanished wife. They had bought it many years ago, for a now (given the state of New York City real estate) ridiculously low sum. As their penthouse had risen in value they had always talked of selling it and buying a house in the country where their gardening joys might really have scope. But the moment had never arrived. The terraces on the penthouse were large, and while Kate Fansler could scarcely tell a lilac from a rhododendron, there was no question even to her ignorant eye that this was an extraordinary rooftop garden. "The house in the country never quite worked out," Tom said when they were once again seated on the terrace after the tour. Kate, looking over the Hudson River to New Jersey, and sipping the iced tea that Tania's husband had served them, did not try to hide her scrutiny of him. Tom was in that state of calm which follows upon terrible news, but also in the state where talk is necessary and all but ceaseless. Kate, glad to serve as an audience to one who would be helped simply by talking, also needed to learn all he could tell her, which was the story of his and Tania's life.

"We would have had to trade this"—his arm swept to indicate the whole terrace with its rich plant life—"for a small apartment and a house, and somehow the whole thing never fell into place. God knows we had great offers for this place, but when we looked at the small apartments we could by then afford, we began to feel cabined, cribbed, and confined, as Hamlet said, before we had even tried it out. And with a house in the country, Tania would have been there only weekends and in the summer. So we just kept talking about it. Now, without her . . ." He did not complete the sentence.

"It was Macbeth," Kate said. "Hamlet talked about being bounded in a nutshell. When did you retire?"

"Five years ago," Tom said. "I was a professor at City College, and I just couldn't take it anymore, teaching remedial English and being mugged in the parking lot. A lot of us took early retirement when the system, in order to get rid of us, made it especially attractive. And it wasn't really the remedial English and the parking lot, it was just that I'd been at the same game too long. As you can see, I've even forgotten my Shakespeare—not that I've taught him since open admissions."

"Have you enjoyed the retirement, until this came along?"

"Moderately. The days pass. I like working around the house. I have a few investments, and they need looking after. I've always wanted to write a novel, but having all day isn't particularly conducive to creation, or so I've found. Funny thing, though, I discovered I really liked cooking. Tania always said she was the oldest kitchen boy in town. We had people in a lot, for dinner, drinks out here. It was a good life. Regular. It doesn't make any sense."

"What do you mean by 'regular'?"

"Every day was just like every other. Well, not exactly, of course. The days Tania taught were different from the days when she didn't teach. We joked: if Tania's teaching Chekhov, it must be Tuesday. And then, every afternoon, when she'd come back from the university—she taught in the morning, and advised from one to three—or just when the hour came round, on the days she didn't teach, she'd take her walk. Down Riverside Drive, across Seventy-second Street to Broadway, down Broadway to Fifty-ninth, and across to Fifth Avenue. Then she'd turn and come back, without the carrots."

"Carrots?"

"For the horses, the ones that pull the carriages through the park. For tourists, I suppose. Tania loved to offer them a carrot each, brightening their lives. It's funny how it began, really; she told me." Tom seemed lost in thought.

"How?" Kate urged him.

"She was crossing Fifty-ninth one day, going some-where—I mean, not on her exercise walk—and a little girl got out of the carriage she was riding in with her family, to have her picture taken with the horse, and she tried to feed the horse a carrot, holding it upright, by its end. Of course the horse took hold of her hand too, and the girl, screaming, dropped the carrot. To the rescue, Tania. She showed the girl how to hold her hand flat with the carrot on it, and calmed her down, although, Tania said, she couldn't convince the child to try again. That's what put the idea of carrots for the horses in Tania's mind. Also, it gave her a destination for her walk, and made it possible for her to say: 'I walk almost three miles every day—warding off osteoporosis and other dangers of aging.' "

Tom fell into a sort of trance, staring out over the Hudson River. "I've been thinking," he finally said, "how we work so hard to avoid the dangers of old age, now that we all live so long, and then, suddenly, we're gone."

"There's no real evidence she's 'gone,' " Kate said.

"I can't believe she wouldn't have let me know, if she was able to. Something terrible must have happened."

"You've been married a long time then," Kate said, not making it a question.

"We were married in the war. We both finished graduate school, and then the children were born. Tania taught all through those years; we needed the money. It was a busy life, but a good one. The children keep calling," he added, reminded of them. "I've gotten to dread the phone calls: 'No news, Pop?' And I always have to say, 'No news.' She can't just have disappeared into thin air," he concluded, in an unconscious echo of Fred Monson.

"What have the police done?" Kate asked, more to have something to ask him than because she needed to be told. The police had put Tania on their missing persons computer, and had made inquiries—perfunctory, Kate felt sure. There had been no ransom notes, no signs at all. Either she was dead—though in that case where was the body?—or she had chosen to vanish. The police admitted that, in the case of aging wives, the latter was unlikely. Amnesia? Possibly. But the hospitals had received no one of that sort, nor had the shelters for the homeless. Weren't there a lot of homeless women on the streets? God knows, there were, and one could hardly question all of them, though most of them were well-enough known in their neighborhoods. Still, no one was likely to report a new bag lady. The police shrugged, officially and metaphorically. Call them when there was a body.

After a while, Kate ran out of questions and Tom fell into silence. She left him finally with sympathetic reassurances, but without much hope on either side.

Later that week, Kate called the chair of the department, Fred Monson, and told him that frankly she didn't think there was much she could do. Just for the hell of it, Kate had walked Tania's exercise route, but no inspiration followed. It was a rainy day, and there were not many horse carriages lined up, just a few across from the Plaza, the horses, under their blankets, looking sad, and the drivers, under their raincoats, looking sullen. Kate liked walking; otherwise she felt a fool.

Fred Monson was not in the best of humors when Kate reached him, and he told her, far from tactfully, that she had been their last hope but not, as far as he was concerned, a very likely one. He'd been told she had a reputation as a detective, but in his view detectives had their being exclusively between the covers of books highly suspect as to quality. Only Dostoyevsky had been able to write intelligently of crime, and he showed you the murder taking place—no nonsense about clues. Kate wanted to say she vaguely remembered a detective in that novel, but resisted the impulse.

"Well," Monson said, "I'll have to hire a substitute for her in the fall if she isn't back by the end of this semester. I've got an assistant professor teaching her classes, but it's hardly fair to anyone. Do let me know," he added unkindly, "if you're inspired with any knowledge of her whereabouts. I certainly hope she returns, but I don't mind telling you, it's the uncertainty that's killing us all." And that was the end of the story as far as anyone knew.

Then, just about at the end of that semester, Tania called Fred Monson and said she was back, she'd just been away awhile, and she'd be teaching and everything as usual in the fall semester. Naturally, Fred wanted to know where she'd been, and how she was. But she wouldn't say much, just that she was back, and that it was good to see Tom, who was glad to have her back, and that the children were also relieved, and they could all now forget the whole thing and enjoy their summer. Except, Tania added, Fred ought to call Kate Fansler and thank her, and apologize for being such a prick (obviously Tania's language hadn't been changed by her absence), because it was due to Kate she was back. She was never, Tania announced, going to say another word about it, but she didn't think Fred ought to have sneered at Kate as a detective. Kate didn't identify with criminals, like the detective in Dostoyevsky and other deep types, but she was damn good, and Fred might as well say so. Fred did write Kate a rather gracious letter, and that was that for a long while. It was only many years later, when Kate told me about Tania, that I learned the part of the story nobody else had ever been told.

TANIA AND FRED were both killed in a car crash years after Tania had retired, and it was when Kate heard that she finally told me the whole story. Kate doesn't often fall into a reminiscent, storytelling vein, but she did that day.

Kate said it was the most patient, foot-slogging work she'd ever done. I like this case because I think only Kate could have solved it. Policemen and tough guy detectives don't bother with cases where they haven't got a body and at least five suspects with a bellyful of hate. That's what made this the perfect Fansler case. At least, pointing that out was how I got Kate to let me publish it.

Somehow, Kate kept finding herself across from the Plaza, studying the horse-drawn carriages. She seemed to have developed a new consciousness of the things: they stopped being a familiar background and moved into the foreground of her awareness. Many years earlier, she and Reed, when they were newly met, had hired one of the carriages and tried to imitate the proper romantic attitudes connected with them. (Reed is now Kate's husband, a word she loathes, but after all a fact is a fact.) They had ended up dissolved in laughter, at their own antics and the prattle of the driver, who took them for newlyweds and tourists, pointing out features of Central Park that Kate had known since birth. The ride had cost five dollars, which indicated how long ago that had been. The notices on the carriages Kate observed informed the romantic and unwary that the price was seventeen dollars for the first quarter hour. Despite these prices, business was good, to judge from the number of carriages lined up, especially on the weekends.

On a warm, spring weekday afternoon Kate hired one. The driver was a young girl in a top hat, her blonde hair seeming to pour out below it to the middle of her back. Kate had approached the girl because she looked, somehow, easier than the male drivers to induce into conversation as opposed to barker talk. Her other attraction was that she had tacked onto the front of her carriage a neat placard announcing that she took American Express cards. The combination of the girl's attractiveness and Kate's lack of cash clinched the matter.

"I'm not a tourist," Kate said, when they had turned off into the park at Sixth Avenue. "I really wanted to ask you about driving these things. It looks like every child's dream, of course. Do most of the drivers like horses? Do they always drive the same horse?"

"Even tourists ask that," the girl said, smiling to make the words pleasant. "Some of us do, some of us don't, to both questions. Mostly we drive the same horse, but if we aren't going to be out, someone else takes over, on a weekend, say. I always try to drive this horse; her name, though you might never guess, is Nellie. She's one of the few mares; mostly they're geldings."

"Do any of you own your horses?"

"Not many anymore. You writing a book or something?"

"Not even 'or something,' " Kate said. "I've just got interested."

"Why don't I give you the usual spiel without your having to ask the questions? Would that help?"

Kate laughed, sitting back, enjoying the slower pace and the sound of the hoofs on the road. The park was closed to cars in the afternoon, and the forsythia was out. Kate couldn't think why she hadn't done this before. Because, she guessed, one thought of it only as a couple or family thing, while it was (though she saw not a single other carriage with only one person in it) an ideal solitary experience. Kate asked for the "usual spiel."

"We all keep our horses in the same stable, the carriages too. There's a good bit of turnover in drivers. As I said, we like horses, or if we don't we pretend to; it would never do to be mean to a horse in the public eye, and we're always in the public eye—that last was not part of the usual spiel, as I'm sure you've guessed. There are rules governing the treatment of the horses. On the hottest days in summer, they can't stay out too long, and they have to have water, and blankets in the winter. People worry a lot more about the horses than the drivers—I don't usually say that either."

"There's a novel by Aldous Huxley," Kate said, "in which some animal lovers take an ill-treated horse away from the man who works it, and as a result he starves to death together with his family. Nobody notices that."

"You a professor or something?"

"Do only professors read?" Kate asked.

"Nobody ever mentioned a book to me before, at least, not a book like that. In the summer when there're more carriages to go out, we get some guys from college as drivers. They don't last very long, but they've read a book.

Probably some of the customers are readers, but they don't
have books on their minds. You'd be surprised what goes
on in these carriages sometimes, particularly at night–I
mean people make out anywhere. I like a little privacy
myself, but it all goes with the territory, I guess. Anything
else I can tell you? This trip's going to cost you already."

Kate agreed to return, and watched the driver pull out
her charge card machine and then write out Kate's
charges. Kate signed the slip, adding a generous tip.
"Thanks a heap," the young woman said. "Any time."

"Do many people feed the horses carrots?" Kate asked,
as an afterthought, pocketing her receipt.

"A lot. Occasional children, though mostly they don't
know how, and old ladies who are pretty regular about it.
People used to feed the horses sugar, which was bad for
them, although they loved it of course. But the new diet
mania in America has helped horses: most people don't
seem to have lumps of sugar anymore; it's more carrots
now, much better for the horses."

Kate thanked her again. "It's been a pleasure meeting
you," she said. "I may be back." And she was, the next
day, and the day after that.

Kate got into the way of coming almost every afternoon
with carrots for the horses, and sometimes an apple. After
a while, she began to distinguish between the horses and to
recognize the drivers, who tolerated her and even greeted
her, a not untypical female animal lover of the sort they
found familiar. But this one distinguished herself by occa-
sionally hiring a carriage and taking a ride, not often, but
often enough to keep hopes and tolerance high. The
regular carrot ladies never rode.

Kate, of course, could come only in the afternoon, and
not every day. Unlike amateur detectives, whether the

effete upper-class English variety or the tough American kind, Kate had a full-time job. I've never really understood what a professor does who teaches only four to six hours a week, though Kate tried to explain it to me once. There are committee meetings and office hours and the need to go on writing and publishing and presenting papers at conferences. That spring, though, Kate devoted a lot of time to horse-drawn carriages. She's an animal lover, like all the Fanslers—I sometimes think it's all she and I share with the rest of the family—and she became quite fond of the horses after a couple of weeks.

There was one driver she noticed, indeed everyone noticed, who worked almost every day, including weekends, and who stood out because he dressed up for the part. He looked exactly like a cabbie from a Sherlock Holmes movie. He wore a black suit, a white tie and shirt, and a top hat. You almost expected someone to get into his carriage, hit the roof (there wasn't any roof, of course) with his cane and say: "Victoria Station, driver, and hurry." Kate took a ride with him one day. This was not as easy as it sounds, because you couldn't just pick out the carriage and driver you wanted. They lined up in order, and you had to take the next one. Kate thought free enterprise would have been better demonstrated if the customers were allowed to choose their carriages. Certainly the competition would have spruced up the carriages and done something for the drivers' appearance; most of them wore old pants and T-shirts, which is what made the elegant man so noticeable. He probably would have had all the customers if the customers had had the choice.

But one day, when Kate came and began her offer of carrots to the horses, the "Edwardian" driver, as she had come to think of him, was third in line. So she sauntered along, feeding and greeting the horses, and chatting with the drivers, until her man was first. Then she hired him.

His spiel turned out to be as unusual as his costume. He began by wishing her good day, and asking if she had any place she especially wanted to see. When Kate said no, just around the park, the driver asked if she would prefer that he talked or kept silent. "And if I keep silent, ma'am," the driver said, with, Kate was amused to notice, just the hint of a cockney accent—one expected him to say "right you are, Gov'ner," but of course he didn't—"I'll still be here to answer questions, if any."

"I'd rather hear what you have to say," Kate said, leaning back.

"Righto, ma'am," he said, turning sideways in his seat so that he could talk to Kate and at the same time keep an eye on the road and the horse. "There's been a carousel here for over a hundred years; they give the horses a bit of paint every so often, and change the tunes. Forty years ago they still had rings you caught as you went by, silver rings but one gold, and if you got the gold, they gave you a free ride." The man seemed to embrace all the park as he spoke of it, as though it were his creation; certainly it was his special pride.

"How long have you been driving a carriage?" Kate asked.

"Oh, most of my life, ma'am, one way or another. I was driving in the park before they ever closed it to cars. I remember when people were married at the Plaza, and they would have a horse-drawn carriage ready to start them on their honeymoon. There were fewer of us in those days, and a different type, ma'am, if you take my meaning. I sometimes try to imagine what New York was like when there were only horse-drawn vehicles about."

"It probably smelled of horse manure, and not carbon

monoxide," Kate said, sitting back and enjoying herself as the description of the passing park scene continued. She didn't interrupt with any more questions; she mused. Wherever Kate is, if she's into musing, she muses. I like to think of her riding around the park on that spring day.

In the end Kate paid the driver with cash; he did not have a charge card notice on his carriage, and Kate had come equipped with enough cash. "I like the way you drive," Kate said. "Is there a time I can come when I'll be fairly certain of getting you?"

"This is a good day," he said. I think it was a Tuesday. "If you come about the same time you did today, we ought to connect. Sometimes business is brisker than other times, so you might miss me, or you might have to wait. The other drivers are all good chaps," he added.

"I'm sure they are," Kate said. "I like your top hat and your line of patter, and your spruced-up carriage. Maybe I'll try again."

And she did try again, a week later. The spring semester was coming to a close, and Kate had to all but walk out on a meeting to get to Central Park South in plenty of time. It was not a particularly fine day, and the "Edwardian" driver was fourth from the head of the line. Kate sat on a bench with the other drivers—those were the only benches on that block—and corrected term papers while she was waiting. To her astonishment, she looked up to see "her" driver pulling his horse out of the rank of waiting carriages and driving off. Kate leapt into the carriage at the head of the line. "Follow that carriage!" she said to the driver.

"What? The horse-drawn one?"

"Yes. Hurry!"

"I can't follow him, lady. He's off back to the stables. I can't take no customers there."

"For a hundred dollars?"

"I might make an exception," he said, whipping up the horse. "But I want to see it."

Kate leaned forward and handed him three twenties. She'd really learned about cash and horse-drawn carriages. This was no moment for American Express, even if it had been the blonde young lady. "Here's sixty. You'll get the other forty when we're there."

But, as it happened, they soon caught up with Kate's "Edwardian" driver, who pulled over and acknowledged defeat, more with a gesture than anything. Cars started honking. Kate handed her driver the other forty, thanked him, got into the "Edwardian" driver's carriage and said: "Back to the park, my good man." The man had to go around the block to Sixth Avenue and head back toward the park. Kate waited until they were through the traffic and back on the park road.

"Why did you take off like that?" Kate asked.

"It was the papers you were correcting, waiting for me. They rang a bell, somehow. Suddenly, I remembered having heard about you and knew who you were. They hired you, I guess."

"I wouldn't say 'hired,' " Kate said. "I haven't promised anything. I can forget I ever rode in a carriage. I've forgotten less forgettable things."

"After all your trouble?"

"No trouble; a pleasure, in fact. And I remembered the gold rings. My brothers used to brag about knowing how to get them. They were already gone in my day. Is this the life you want really, from now on? And of course, there's Tom."

"What made you guess?"

"Lots of things–his quoting Macbeth mainly, though he thought it was Hamlet. Hamlet may really have been closer: 'I could be bounded in a nutshell, and count myself a king of infinite space, were it not that I have bad dreams.' Was that it, or was it Macbeth: 'cabined, cribbed, confined'?"

"You mean you understand?"

"Lord, yes. But most of us don't have a dream to step into; we don't have a job to go to."

"I got to know this old man who drove. Met him when I was feeding the horses. I've always loved horses, not race-horses or riding horses or herding horses, but horses that pull carriages. He wanted to quit, and I offered him enough for his carriage and horse really to tempt him, if he could get them for me and the right to keep them where he did, to live where he did, right close to the stables. He said at first he couldn't manage it, but in the end he did. I was offering to exchange my escape for his, and I knew it would work if I was patient."

"Is that his suit?"

"No. This outfit is all mine. He was a much smaller man, wizened and disillusioned about the carriages working the park these days."

"What about Tom? The worry it's been to him?"

"He's been worried, but I bet he's also felt alive: something to think about, to plan beyond. It's brought a change to his life too; it was getting too predictable. As to the department . . ."

"I know," Kate said, "they can all pee up one rope. When will you decide about going back? Not that I want to rush you."

"Once more around the park, on me."

And so they rode around in silence. The evening was drawing in. "You mean I have a real choice," the driver said, looking back at her, and when Kate nodded, turned around and continued driving in silence. Until they were leaving the park:

"Mine has been such an orderly life," Tania said. "I

married when my mother and everyone else thought I should—not that it wasn't a good marriage. We had children at the right time; they were good children. I guess working was the only unusual thing I did, and of course I became a language teacher, which was okay for a woman. Somehow, except when I was very young, there wasn't time for a dream, for an adventure. Suddenly, this seemed the perfect thing. A carriage, a horse, an outfit."

"You weren't afraid of being recognized?"

"Not in this outfit. People see what they expect to see. And I've always had a deep voice and a flat chest. Very good legs, though," Tania added.

When they pulled up at the curb on Central Park South, Kate said: "I get off here. I understand more than you'll ever know about how you felt. You decide it the way you want. I shan't say a word to anyone. And I won't bother you with any more rides, if you decide to stay with the carriages and horses. But if you decide to go back, just call your Chair, dear Fred Monson, and announce your return for next semester. 'Never apologize, never explain.' A good Victorian piece of advice."

AS YOU KNOW, Tania decided to return. And from that day to this, no one ever knew where she'd been, and no one ever guessed. They were all glad to see her back—Tom, and the students, and even her colleagues—so she found out she was loved. Maybe that made her return more rewarding. But Kate never knew, because Kate never spoke to her again.

ONCE UPON A TIME

⌖

This was the only true story she had ever heard, Kate Fansler used to say, that properly began "once upon a time." Kate, who had never seen the beginning, said it was, nonetheless, as clear to her inner eye as any personal memory, sharp in all its detail, as immediate as sense itself. The family to whom it happened was named Grant. They were in their summer home in New England. "The King was in the counting house, counting out his money; the Queen was in the parlor, eating bread and honey." That is, the father, as in this context we should call him, had gone into town for the papers; he had money invested, and wanted to study the stock market pages. The mother, a college professor, was upstairs in her study, ostensibly writing an article for a conference on the uses of fantasy, in fact, reading a novel by Thomas Hardy, which seemed—as she later said, sounding prophetic—to answer to her condition. The children were on the lawn playing a ragged and hilarious game of volleyball.

There were four of them, three boys and a girl, all twelve years of age. The girl and one of the boys were twins; the other two boys were school friends, come for the weekend. They too were twins, identical as opposed to their fraternal twin hosts, and the badminton set had been their hostess's gift. They had been invited for two weeks, as a favor to their parents, and because the resident twins were judged too self-reliant and in need of outside stimulation. It had taken a whole day to put up the posts for the net, and another day to practice with the rackets and shuttlecocks. The father had pointed out that they could play volleyball with the same net, and had, the next afternoon, provided the ball.

There the four of them were, having both learned and invented the game, playing at it furiously and with much shouting–the girl was as good at it as the boys, and taller than the visiting twins–when one of the visiting twins (they do not remain in this story long enough to be named) shouted: "Look! It's a baby!"

And, as the four of them would remember the scene and tell of it for the rest of their lives, a baby, wearing a diaper and shirt and nothing else, came toddling toward them out of the bushes that lined the property and across the lawn. The baby was about a year and a half old and appeared to have learned to walk only recently. It rocked toward them, with that unsteady gait characteristic of babies, and laughed, holding out its arms, probably for balance but, as it seemed, reaching toward them. And what seemed most marvelous, it chortled in that wonderful way of babies, with little yelps of delight as it staggered toward them.

The volleyball players ran down the lawn toward the baby. An adult, or even the sort of twelve-year-old girl who played house and dreamed of herself in a bridal gown, would have scooped up the baby. These children simply stood one on either side of her—which two took the baby's hands could never, afterward, be agreed upon; perhaps they took turns—and slowly moved, midst coos of encouragement, toward the house. The girl then ran ahead—allowing a boy to take the baby hand she held, or so she insisted—to alert their mother. "Ma," she called. "A baby walked out of the bushes."

The professor, reading of how Clym Yeobright's mother died, returned to the New England summer afternoon with difficulty. "What do you mean?" she is reported to have said, rather crossly. (The story had been retold so often that parts of it became "authentic," as other parts continued to be debated.) She was dragged by her daughter to the window—after having returned her eyes to her book as though her daughter had merely said, "An elephant with wings has landed on the lawn"—where she witnessed the baby's progress toward the house, its hands being held by two attentive boys.

"Where did it come from?" she not unreasonably asked.

"Just out of the bushes," her daughter answered. The professor rushed downstairs and out onto the road: there was no sign of any car or person. Their house was at the end of a dirt road, and any car or person on the road was clearly visible.

"Did you hear a car?" the professor asked. By this time she had reached the baby and held out her arms: the baby walked into them. The professor held and smelt the baby, and put its cheek to hers, as she had not done with her own children; there had been two, which had (as she admitted only to herself and the mother of the visiting twins) doubled the work while halving those intense moments of a mother and baby alone in the entire world.

"We didn't hear anything," the children all said, jumping around her. "Of course we would have heard a car if there had been one." This was so obviously true, the professor argued no further. Someone must somehow have crept along the side of the road, set the baby toddling toward the children, and crept away.

"What did you think of when you saw the baby and heard that story?" the professor was often asked.

"I thought of Moses," she always answered. "And, of course, of Silas Marner."

This latter allusion turned out to be, on the whole, the more appropriate. The baby was a girl, as they discovered after the father, returning with his papers, had been immediately dispatched back to town for diapers and baby food. The mother with three of the children, the fourth being left downstairs with the baby, searched the attic for a portable crib that had been retained from earlier years, for the possible use of visiting young. When the father returned, and they had changed and fed the baby, they all sat down at the table, the parents with a stiff drink, and discussed the matter.

"We could advertise," one of the children said. "Or put up a notice. Like they do with lost cats and dogs." Everyone laughed but, as the parents were quick to point out, no one had a better suggestion. And then the father looked at the professor and said: "Geraldine and Tom."

"Of course," the mother and the home twins said. "But," the children asked, "couldn't we keep her?"

"Our arms are full," the professor said happily. "Besides," she added, "if we'd wanted anyone else, we would have her by now. Our family is complete."

"Geraldine and Tom then," the home twins said, not really disagreeing with their mother. "But," the girl twin added, "she did seem to choose us."

"That's because we were playing on the lawn," her twin said. "It seems a good place where children are playing on the lawn."

"We'll have to tell that to Geraldine and Tom," the father said.

And that was where the "once upon a time" part of the story ended. The professor went away to call Geraldine and Tom, who immediately drove up from New York and looked at the baby as though she had indeed dropped from the skies. "It was *much* better than that," the children insisted. And they had to tell the story again, the first repeat of many. After that, it was courts and judges and social workers and the long, slow process of the law.

GERALDINE AND TOM, who might as well be known as the Rayleys, were friends of the Grants. Tom was a corporate lawyer who had made partner five years ago, and was wildly successful and overworked. Geraldine ran an elegant clothing shop. Unlike those who discovered late in their thirties that they wanted a child, the Rayleys had always wanted one, but it had just never happened. Only lately, consulting doctors and learning that there was no evident reason for their failure, had they decided to adopt. Here they immediately ran into trouble: they were too old and they were of different religions, to mention only the major points emphasized by the adoption agencies. The other markets for babies they had not tried. Tom was one of those whom anything even touching upon the illegal or shady disgusted: he was a person of almost flaming rectitude and integrity, which, as the Grants used to point out to each other, was a pretty odd thing in a corporate lawyer, dearly as the Grants loved the Rayleys. Geraldine and Tom's desire for a baby seemed to swell with the passing years, almost, the professor used to say, as a mother's body swells with the growing baby inside her. Afterward, many people were to remark how amazingly simple-minded the Grants had been. They had a baby who had toddled toward them out from the mountain laurel. They had friends who longed for a baby. What could be more logical than, pending discovery of the baby's provenance, bringing them all together? "But," people would say later, hearing the story, "the disappointment later for the Rayleys if the baby's mother had been found."

"It was all we could think to do," the professor would say when this point was made. "We all seemed to be acting as though we were in some fairy story. Well, we were in a fairy story. And it did work out, so we did the right thing, Q.E.D."

For the Rayleys, after many years' experience of the law's delay, got to keep the baby. They adopted her legally, but even before that, she was registered for the best school in New York, which Geraldine had attended; she spent her earliest years as a Rayley at an excellent nursery school. The baby, whom they named Caroline, remained as she had first appeared, a laughing, happy child. With adolescence she grew more serious and seemed oddly dissatisfied with her richly endowed life. Fortunately, her parents, as one might expect of a man of Tom's principles and a woman who endorsed them, were not advocates of material indulgence for children. Caroline was kept on a strict allowance, and had to account for her evenings. Her parents were of a liberal persuasion, however, and despite all the horrors reported daily of adolescent extravagances, they and Caroline always got on. She went away to college and, eventually, to graduate school. In time, she became an assistant professor at a university in New York. That, of course, was where she met Kate Fansler.

· · ·

IT WAS, HOWEVER, not Caroline but her father, Tom
Rayley, who first talked to Kate at any length about that
amazing scene on the lawn almost thirty years earlier. Caroline and Kate had become friendly, as happens now and
then with full professors and much younger assistant professors. As Kate would often say, the friendship is not one
of equals, nor can it pretend to be when one friend has
such power, direct or indirect, over the destiny of another.
All the same, they suited one another. Kate was reaching
that difficult point in some lives when, growing older, one
finds one's ideas and hopes more in accord with those of
the young than with those of one's own contemporaries.
Kate's peers seemed to grow more conservative and fearful
as she grew more radical and daring. Not that Kate was
then or ever of the stuff from which revolutionaries are
made. Perhaps because of her fortunate life, her indiffer-
ence—either because she had them or did not desire them—
to many of the goods of life, she seemed not to barricade
herself against disturbing ideas or changing ways. The
same could not, surely, be said of Tom Rayley. He came to
Kate in fear, though he could scarcely tell her of what. Fear
came, he suggested, with his time of life.

"I have turned sixty," he said. "It humbles a man. For
one thing," he added darkly, "the body starts falling apart.
I've never had very much wrong with me, and all of a
sudden I find I have to make a huge effort to hold on to my
teeth; I've got a strange disease of which they know the
name but not a cure; I've also acquired what they call
degenerative arthritis, which turns out to be another term
for old age; and when I got the laboratory report from my
doctor, not only was my cholesterol up, but the lab had
noted, 'serum appears cloudy,' which didn't bother the
doctor but sounded ominous to me. On top of all that, I'd

rather Caroline didn't go off to live with her newfound mother or father in a community somewhere full of strange rites and a profound mistrust of life's conventions."

Kate and Tom Rayley had met when Caroline invited Kate home for dinner. Geraldine, like Tom, lived a life in which the strict control of emotion and the avoidance of untidiness, literal or psychological, were paramount. Highly intelligent, they were good conversationalists, Geraldine in particular offering amusing and revealing accounts of the international world of fashion and the Manhattan world of real estate with which fashion, like everything else, was so intimately connected. Tom seemed rather the sort who takes in information while giving out as little as possible; he was pleasant, but after the dinner Kate realized she knew little or nothing about him.

Only when she had been, to her astonishment, summoned to lunch for a private interview did Kate discover that Tom Rayley was an impressive man, just the sort one would think of as a senior partner in a corporate law firm. Kate wondered if his democratic convictions came from an open mind or from his Southern boyhood at a time when all Southerners were Democrats. Since Rayley had not turned Republican like so many of his sort, and had settled in New York, she gave him the benefit of the doubt: his was an open mind, fearful perhaps of aging and of loneliness, but not of those chimeras requiring for their alleviation belief in nuclear weapons, separation of the races, and the strict domestication of women.

Kate was so astonished at his sudden frankness, helplessness, and revelations that she hardly knew what to say.

"What is the disease with a name but no cure?" she asked without really thinking.

"It's a rather personal male disease, apparently of no

great significance but calculated to detonate every hideous
male fear ever recorded. It's called Peyronie's disease, but
whether he had it, identified it, or dismissed it is unclear.
The only problem once it is diagnosed is–at least in my
case–that my liver responded in a regrettable way to the
drug supposed to alleviate it. I can't imagine why we're discussing this."

"Because it has made you fearful of Caroline's defection.
I have to say," Kate went on, "that children seem to me
notably unsatisfactory when it comes to the question of
their parents. Between those who fantasize other parents
and those who seek biological parents, it seems that no one
is satisfied. Perhaps we ought to follow Plato's suggestion
and have a world where biological parentage is neither
known nor significant."

"I'm perfectly aware that my anxiety is irrational and
illogical. As a lawyer, if not as a practical realist, how could
I not be aware? I think that's why I wanted to talk with
you. You, I surmise, deal in stories like this. Caroline
admires you and will probably speak to you about her
'original appearance' more intently than she has spoken to
anyone else. Also–and I hope you will not desert me
totally at this honesty–I did infer that, as a sister of the
famous Fansler lawyers, you would hardly be, shall we say,
a disruptive person."

"Not disruptive, but not soothing either. I'm very unlike
my brothers in every possible way; perhaps you've heard
that. And if you're expressing some naive belief in genes,
let me point out the inefficacy of that attitude from an
adoptive and loving parent."

"Oh, dear, yes," Tom Rayley said, in no way offended.
"But that's part of my fear, you see. How can I say it? That
Caroline, discovering something, one hardly knows what,

will fall out of our world and into some other world, to me unspeakable. And you, at least so far, while in another world, are not unspeakable. I understand your language; I can even learn it."

Kate stared at him. "That is a remarkably intelligent thing to say," she said. "I'm happy to talk with you, though Caroline is my friend, and I shall certainly talk to her also. But I am bewildered: What can you possibly think I can do for you? Isn't this all between you and your wife and Caroline? Isn't it all about the life you three have had together for all but a year and a half of Caroline's existence?"

"You've heard the story then, the appearance from the bushes of the laughing child?"

"Yes. I've heard it from Caroline. As she's heard it, and as it has been disputed and refined over the years. But she and I have not talked about it, not as you and I are talking now. It's an amazing story certainly. Almost mythic."

"Exactly. It's myths I fear, you see. That's the whole point. I don't mind a bereft mother or even father appearing after all these years. I fear the power of the myth. I was wondering if you could detect it: demythologize it. Isn't that what they do in literary criticism these days?"

"All I can do is talk to Caroline, which I do anyway. And to you, if an intelligent question occurs to me. But where can this lead, except around in the same circles? Caroline isn't desperate for the truth, resting her whole identity and future life on some revelation. Your fears seem excessive."

"They are. They are the fears that come with the youth of senility, as another lawyer once described it. Will you just accept my trepidation as part of your agenda, one of those 'cases' you think about?"

"I can do that certainly," Kate said, half amused, half

fearful of his intensity, inadequately masked. "What of the mother of the twins, the one who was reading Hardy? Is she still alive?"

"Oh yes, still a professor. And she's never moved an inch from the story, nor have her children. It's legend now, it's a truth beyond truth."

KATE HAD INTENDED to mention the conversation with Caroline's father the next day, when she and Caroline walked home together, as was now their custom. They lived within a few blocks of one another but never, to their amusement, met except at the university. Those few blocks separated one New York City neighborhood from another. Caroline, however, mentioned the conversation first. Her father had called her the previous night to report upon the lunch he and Kate had shared. "The general hope, I'm to gather, is that you will come to dinner with the parents from time to time, and head off the effects of any terrible revelation, or the lack of such a revelation, upon their daughter. I hope you don't feel unduly burdened. In the beginning, my appearance from the bushes seemed a good story; I don't know why it has become so fearsome."

"Stories of that sort do," Kate said. "Like the moment after an electrical failure, when the bright lights go on and the candles are scarcely visible, superfluous. Here we are, talking now about your amazing appearance, while before we used to chat on about everything, nothing outshining the rest."

"Do you mind?" Caroline asked.

"Partly. Partly I want to shout out that it doesn't matter how you were born or miraculously shone forth; what matters is that you have a blessed life, and the chance for an interesting future. But then I know that's nonsense.

The question is, shall you be able eventually to forget the story, let it fade into the general history of things, or shall it keep, as they so wonderfully say in criticism today, foregrounding itself?"

"Certainly it will fade if it never changes, never gets any commentary added to it, never gets reinterpreted. Do you think you might be persuaded to go and see Henrietta Grant?"

"The mother of the twins, the one who was reading Hardy? What could I go to see her for? I could hardly request to hear the story again, as one might have asked a bard to recite the lines about Odysseus's meeting with Nausicaa. I mean, if she wants to keep telling it, why not tell it to someone who hasn't heard it before?"

"I don't think she tells it much, or likes to. Mostly others tell it now, her children, me, Mom and Dad. It's just that she's got to be the answer."

"The answer to where you came from?"

"Yes. She's the only one who could possibly know."

"Caroline, that's obviously untrue. Unless she was in two places at once, and nothing in the story allows one to believe that, the only person who can possibly know is the one who set you off toward the volleyball players from behind the bushes and then crept away. And at least with the needle in the haystack, you supposedly know what haystack you lost the needle in."

"You mean someone spotted that house, the children, the geography of the lawn, the dirt road, all of it, and just decided that was a good place to dump a baby."

"That's the likeliest explanation surely."

"Perhaps. Except, Kate, I know I was a happy child, and all that, but if someone the child knows puts her down, is she likely to go running, happily gurgling the while, toward complete strangers in a strange place? I mean, she couldn't have known the children, but mightn't she have known the place?"

"You're looking for a rational explanation, my dear. That is the great temptation with a story like this. As in the Gershwin song, where the Pharaoh's daughter is suspected of being the mother of Moses, the baby *she* found. Surely the whole point about marvelous happenings is that there isn't any explanation, anyway not one that would satisfy a rationalist. I think that's why your father's so worried; he half hopes for a rational explanation, and half fears the lack of one: if you consider yourself miraculous, even miraculously adventurous for a baby, you become otherworldly, part of legend, not simply his child."

"Does that mean I ought to look for a mundane answer, or not?"

"Myself, I'd feel tempted to accept it just as it is: be glad you landed in that place, that your parents were there to claim you when called, that you were born at a later age than most, in an improbable way. It all seems to me a kind of blessing, better than fairy godmothers around your cradle. But who am I to talk, having always known exactly where I came from, and regretting it the greater part of the time? There is, you see, the danger that you will waste your energies on the past, and miss the present and the future. I think that's often a danger, and one worth risking only under the most extreme conditions—total despair or anxiety, for example. What can you learn from the past before you burst upon that volleyball game that's worth knowing? That's what I'd ask myself."

"There's always plain old curiosity."

"So there is. But maybe that's more my problem than yours. After all, I've made curiosity a kind of avocation. If you give me permission, I can promise to be curious enough for both of us."

"Does that mean you might try to discover something?"

"Probably not. It means that I'll go on wondering; you go on living."

"Should your curiosity ever lead to any answers, will you promise to tell me? No, don't protest," Caroline said, as Kate started to speak. "Let's make it a bargain. I'll stop thinking about the whole scene, stop even telling it to new people I meet; I'll just say I'm adopted and let it go at that. I think you're right about the past entrenching itself in the present and future. But if I give up this wonderful question, you have, in turn, to promise to tell me if there ever is an answer. Agreed?"

Kate agreed, and with relief. The story was beginning to frighten her in the hold it was getting on Caroline and Tom Rayley. She called Tom Rayley and told him of the bargain, urging him to forget myths and concentrate on his satisfactory daughter.

And there for a time the matter rested.

THE RESURRECTION OF the myth was an outcome of Kate's meeting with Henrietta Grant. They found themselves together on a panel, both last-minute substitutes; each, it later transpired, had agreed to fill in as a special favor, Henrietta to the remaining panelist, Kate to the man who had organized the panel in the first place. They were introduced five minutes before the panel began, each trying to remember where she had heard the other's name. Both thought of Caroline as the connection during the first paper, and they nodded that recognition to one another as the man's words on the New Historicism in the Renaissance prepared the way for Henrietta on the New Historicism in

French writing of the eighteenth century and for Kate on English writers of the nineteenth.

"Shall we have a drink?" Henrietta asked when they had answered the last of the questions and watched the audience disperse. "Or do you feel duty bound to remain for the next panel?"

"Neither duty bound nor so inclined," Kate answered. "After all, we are substitutes; it's not as though we had signed on for the whole bit. And even if I had, the truth is I would like to have a drink with you." They soon settled themselves in the bar of the hotel where the conference was being held. Kate felt she deserved a martini complete with olive.

"How is Caroline?" Henrietta asked. "I understand working with you has been a real opportunity. Not that I've seen her lately."

"I wouldn't call it an opportunity. We're friends, which is a good thing. The fact is," Kate added, as her martini and Henrietta's Scotch arrived, "I never expected really to meet you, any more than I expected to come upon two sets of twelve-year-old twins playing volleyball. Or upon Huck and Jim on a raft, if it comes to that. Certain scenes live only in the imagination."

"The twins are not *that* much younger than you," Henrietta laughed. "My twins, at least, have turned out rather well. I've lost track of the other two, so they remain always twelve in my mind also. They moved away after that summer."

"I wonder if they tell the story of Caroline's arrival."

"I'm pretty sure they do. They got used to telling it that summer. It's not the sort of story you forget."

"It's all passed into legend by now. How does it feel to be part of a legend?"

"It was an amazing moment. I feel a kind of wonder

about Caroline, as though, after that birth, as amazing and as charming in its way as that of Botticelli's Venus, she was bound to be a marvel, do something that would reverberate, become, in her own way, a myth."

"The birth of the hero, as Raglan and others have it, only this time a woman hero. More Moses than Eppie in *Silas Marner*. And of course the two sets of twins add a note, a kind of amazing circumstance."

"Not really," Henrietta laughed. "Think of the Bobbsey Twins. Just a convenient circumstance." Henrietta looked for a moment down at her hands. "I do hope Caroline's stopped brooding about it. I worry about the Rayleys; I worry about her. Like one of those babies conceived *in vitro*: How can anything in life equal its first moment? I mean, can a life hold two miracles?"

"The whole point of heroic lives is that they do, isn't that so? The miraculous birth, therefore the awful and wonderful destiny. Not that I can imagine that for Caroline, who is such a sane person, which heroes rarely are."

"Male heroes," Henrietta said, and they went on to talk of other things.

But, the ice being broken, they met again from time to time, when Henrietta was in New York or Kate in Boston. And then one spring day Kate, finding herself at Williams College and remembering that Henrietta's country house, on whose lawn Caroline had appeared that long-ago afternoon, was nearby, telephoned on the chance that Henrietta might be there, might ask her to stop by.

"Your sense of geography is rather wonderful," Henrietta remarked. "I'm an hour at least away, and despite the careful directions I shall now give you, you will get lost. Stop and telephone again when you realize you've made a wrong turn. And plan to spend the night if you come at all.

You'll be far too late to drive anywhere today. I'm all alone, so there's plenty of room. I'll put you in the room where I was reading the day Caroline appeared."

Kate did get lost, did call again, did arrive as the day was darkening, the trees beginning to be outlined against the evening sky. Kate drove down the dirt road on which Henrietta's house stood, was shown the bushes that lined the property at its sides, and the lawn where the badminton net had been. Beyond the lawn was woods. The silence was amazing to Kate.

"Come in," Henrietta said. "We'll sit by the fire and lift a glass to Caroline."

"Has she been back here often?" Kate asked.

"Oddly not; the Rayleys visited with her once, but they wouldn't take their eyes off her. I think they feared she would wander off just as she had come, holding out her hands to someone else. It took them years to believe that Caroline was there to stay. They used to go into her room at night to be sure she hadn't vanished into thin air. Eventually Caroline became a real little girl who could be trusted out on her own. Fortunately, she was small when they got her, so she had time to grow into independence and they had time to accept it. The Rayleys are very sound people, which was a great relief."

"You knew that when you called them that day?"

"I knew them well, of course. But all I thought of that day was their longing for a child, and the child's need of a home. I felt, even though I'd just met Caroline, an urgency that she find the right home, not just be adopted by people I'd never heard of, however worthy."

Kate started to ask another question, but restrained herself. The time for questions had passed; the time for answers might come, but only Henrietta could decide that.

They sat with their drinks in front of the fire and let the evening darken altogether before they turned on the lights and thought about dinner.

"I've a thick soup I made last night; it improves with age, like the best women. Will that do? There's also home-made bread and decent wine."

"It sounds like the beginning of another fantasy," Kate said. "I don't get to the country much, and rarely am offered homemade soup and bread. Mostly I subsist on nouvelle cuisine and fish, neither of which I especially like. When we're home we eat omelettes or Chinese food, delivered by an intense young person on a bicycle. This is a lovely change. Can we eat in front of the fire, looking like a scene from a made-for-television movie?"

"We are, I fear, insufficiently rustic."

But nothing else was insufficient. One of those times, Kate thought, when it is all just right, and you never quite understand why, except that it was unplanned and in the highest degree unlikely ever to happen just that way again.

Dinner over, they sat sipping their coffee by the fire, which was dying because Henrietta hesitated to throw on another log: it would commit them to a delayed bedtime. Kate was beyond the most minor decision. It had been a long day, but she was in that odd state of fatigue past weariness. She simply sat. And Henrietta, having, it seemed, decided, threw a large log on the fire.

"I'd better tell you," she said, sitting forward and staring at the fire. "Someone, I suppose, should know. But if I tell you, it will end our friendship. I'll trust you, but I won't want to know you anymore. Which is a pity; the world is not that full of intelligent friends."

Kate couldn't argue with the truth of that. "But if I

say don't tell me, shall we go on being friends? Is it my decision?"

"Probably not," Henrietta said, sighing. "In telling you there was anything to tell, I've already crossed that bridge; I've already burned it."

"It's ironic," Kate said. "Like so much else. I guessed, of course—not what you would tell, but that there was something to tell. Once you knew that, we were destined to have only this one night by the fire."

"Truncated friendships are my fate," Henrietta said. "As you shall learn. There never is any turning back." Henrietta paused only a moment.

"It began with a young woman very like Caroline now, a graduate student. We became friends, as you have with Caroline. But it was, or seemed, a more perilous friendship then. Women didn't become close to one another; their eyes were always on the men. I was an associate professor, rather long in the tooth for that, but women didn't get promoted very rapidly in those days. We talked, this graduate student and I, about, oh, everything I seemed never to have talked about. Such talk became more ordinary later, with CR groups and all the rest; it's hard now to recall the loneliness of professional women in those years, the constant tension and anxiety of doing the wrong thing, of offending.

"You have to understand what a conservative woman I was then. If I felt any criticism of the academic world I had fought my way into, I never let it rise to consciousness, let alone expressed it. I just wanted to be accepted, to teach, to write; I liked to tell myself it was simple. And my life was very full. There were the twins; there was my marriage, good then, better now, fine always— we've worked on it, examined our assumptions. But to understand this story you have to imagine yourself back then, back before Betty Friedan described 'the problem that has no name.'

"I asked my new friend to the country, alone, just as you are here tonight. The children stayed in Boston with their father; he was good about helping me to get away, now and then. And they were all involved in Red Sox games and other things I could never pretend interest in. He thought it might be good for me to talk to someone; 'girl-talk,' he called it. None of us had any decent language for women friends." And Henrietta stopped and began to cry, not loudly, no noise at all. The tears fell silently. "Maybe you can guess the rest," she said.

Kate nodded. "She misunderstood, or you did. She made what used to be called a 'pass.' Today I think they would say she came on to you. Were you terrified?"

"It isn't even right to call it a pass. It was a gesture of love. I can see that now. Then, I simply went rigid with terror. And that's what I felt: sheer, paralyzing terror. I knew nothing about women loving women, except that I feared it; we had been taught to fear it. My terror was obvious."

"And she ran away?"

"No. She didn't run. We went on with the evening—we'd arrived in late afternoon—we went on with dinner, we 'made' conversation. I never really understood the agony of that phrase until then. Somewhere in her diaries Woolf talks of beating up the waves of conversation. We did that. Nothing helped; not wine, not food. We said nothing that mattered. The next morning she was gone."

"Gone from graduate school too?"

"Yes. I had no idea where she was, or what had become of her. I tried, discreetly of course, to find out, but she seemed simply to have vanished. The way graduate students do vanish, from time to time. Sometimes they surface again, sometimes not. Once in a while—and this is what terrified me most—they kill themselves."

"But she went off and had an affair with a man."

"You seem to know the story. Is it as ordinary as all that?"

"Not a bit. One doesn't need to be a detective to guess the next step as you tell it. You've just kept it a secret so long."

"It was such a daring plot, you see. I didn't ever want to wreck the magic of that scene by telling anyone. It succeeded beyond my wildest hopes."

"You planned it."

"Of course. She was very clear about not wanting the baby, as she had been clear about having it. A rarely honest woman, for that time. She adored the child, but recognized her impatience, her lack of desire to be a mother, let alone a single mother. She had never told the father she was pregnant; she never told me who he was. I keep saying how different it all was in those days: you have to remember that.

"Caroline was a magic child; that made the plot easier. One of those children who are friendly, open, who greet all the world with delight. I made excuses to visit the country house alone; it wasn't hard. I had work to do, and my husband knew the summer with the children here and guests was not an easy time for intense work. Caroline was brought here secretly, for a short time each day; I played with her. A game. I was in the house; Caroline was put down by the bushes, and she came toward the house to find me. It's simple, isn't it, when you know?"

"Did your husband know?" Kate asked.

"No. I was terribly tempted to tell him, but it was clear he would play his part better if he didn't know it was a part. His being off the scene was just chance; I didn't plan that."

Kate thought about it awhile. "And your friend," she finally asked, "what became of her?"

"She died. In some freak accident–it was horrible. I heard only later, by chance. All the time she was here with the child, she never melted, never said anything meaningful beyond 'Help me' in the beginning, and, just before the end, 'Goodbye.' She crept off through the woods as Caroline moved toward the twins."

"Your plot worked more perfectly than most plots. Like magic."

"Just like magic. I didn't even know the Rayleys would be reached immediately that day, would come so soon. That afternoon's legend has always seemed to me to have some of the qualities of a Homeric hymn. But before and after the afternoon, that's the sorrow. We never made it up; she never forgave me."

Kate could find nothing to say except "There's Caroline."

"Yes," Henrietta answered. "And she's your friend. Neither of you is my friend."

"That can always change," Kate said. "Maybe this time, you'll find the words to change all that."

"Don't tell Caroline," Henrietta said. "Don't tell anyone."

"No," Kate said. "But I shall be breaking a promise to Caroline. I promised to tell her if there was ever an answer. Perhaps one day you will let me keep that promise, or you will keep it for me."

"Perhaps. But there are no parents for Caroline to find."

"There is a friendship between two women when that

was rare enough. And there is the magic afternoon. That's more than most of us begin with."

Henrietta only shook her head. And after a time, she went to bed, leaving Kate by the fire. In the morning, before Kate left, Henrietta spoke cheerfully of other things. The sun was not yet bright on the lawn as Kate drove away.

ARRIE AND JASPER

∽

My aunt Kate Fansler doesn't care for children. I'm her niece, but I never really got to know her till we ran into each other when I was a student at Harvard. It's true my cousin Leo spent a summer with her, and lived with her a year or so when he was in high school, but he wasn't really a child in high school, and during that summer she had a hired companion for him and sent him to day camp besides. Kate Fansler always refused to become defensive about this. "I don't much like children," she admitted. "I know it's an eccentric attitude, but not a dangerous one. The worst fate I've ever inflicted on any child is to avoid it. As it happens, however," she added, "I did once more or less solve a case for a child. Do you think that will serve to redeem me in the eyes of those with maternal instincts?"

Kate was in her office at the university, about to conclude that her office hour was over and the thought of a martini with Reed could be realistically contemplated, when she heard a timid knock. Kate looked through the glass in the top half of her door and saw a silhouette reaching only a few inches above where the glass began. A midget, she thought. Well, midgets have problems too. But do they have academic problems, and with me? She opened the door to find herself confronting a girl child wearing a school uniform, glasses, braces, and a frown. Kate stared at the child so long, she asked if she might come in. Kate apologized and ushered her in, closing the door.

"Forgive me," Kate said. "I was just a bit startled. You look rather young for graduate school. Or even for college, if it comes to that. Are you lost?"

"I've come to hire you as a detective," the child said. "I have money. My father says you probably couldn't find a herd of buffalo in a field covered with snow, but I figure if he doesn't like you, you must be good."

"My dear young woman," Kate said, dropping back into the chair behind her desk, "I don't know which misapprehension to confront first. But, in the order in which you offered them: I'm not a detective, either private or police; they work at that job a lot harder than I do; I have detected from time to time, but I never take money, it might cloud the fine, careless rapture of the adventure; I don't know who your father is; and I am somewhat concerned that you hold his opinion in such low regard."

You might think all this verbiage would have frightened the kid, but she held her ground admirably. "I hope I didn't offend you about the money," she said, returning her wallet to her pocket. "I would be very glad of your help."

"It doesn't sound to me as though your father would approve of your seeking my help, nor of my offering it. Who is your father? Someone I know?"

"His name is Professor Witherspoon," the child said, assured that his name was sufficient to establish his identity and credentials in Kate's eyes. She was quite right. Witherspoon was a member of Kate's department, and to say that he and Kate never saw eye to eye on anything was to put their relationship in its least emotional terms. Kate was frank to admit that she could never decide if he was a monster or a lunatic; the best that could be said on her side was that most of the department agreed with her. Kate eyed his progeny with some dismay.

"It sounds to me as though I'm the last person you should come to. Am I to gather that your dislike of your father is sufficient to recommend to you someone he despises?"

The kid had no trouble with this one either, merely nodding. "I think he's the most awful man I know," she added. "I didn't come to you just for that reason, though. My sister took a class with you, and she considered you worthy of recommendation."

"Well," Kate said with some relief, "I'm glad to hear there is one member of your family that you like. But I can't say I ever remember having a Witherspoon in my class. I don't remember all my students' names, but I have a feeling I would have noticed hers."

"Roxanna has taken our mother's name: Albright. I'm going to do the same as soon as I can. I'll have to wait at least until I leave high school. My sister is a lot older than me; she's very smart and very beautiful, not like me."

"You look fine to me," Kate said. She meant it. Kate is the best disregarder of beauty in any conventional sense I've ever met, and if a person is glamorous or studiously well-dressed, they have to go a long way to gain her trust.

"I don't look like my mother," the child said with evident regret. "Also, I'm strabismic and have an overbite.

Put differently," she added, "my eyes have difficulty focusing on the same object, and my upper and lower jaws fail to meet properly. I think it's because I was such a disappointment. I was unexpected, you see, but they hoped—that is, my father hoped—that at least I would be a boy. I wasn't," she added sadly, in case Kate had any doubt.

Had the kid but known it, she had picked the quickest way to Kate's sympathies. I think Kate asked her what she wanted in order to get her off the topic of her drawbacks.

"I want you to find my dog," the kid said.

About this time, I'm sure, Kate was beginning to think of that martini with something close to passion. "I wouldn't know how to begin to look for a lost dog in this city," she said. "I'm afraid it may have been snatched by someone, or else wandered off and was hit by a car. Have you tried the ASPCA?"

"He wasn't lost; he was stolen. And not on the streets, out of the apartment. The doorman saw someone leaving with Jasper under his arm. And the apartment wasn't broken into. Which means it was an inside job."

Kate took the bull by the horns (the same bull Witherspoon no doubt would think her capable of overlooking in a china shop). "Do you suspect your father?" she asked.

"I don't know who to suspect." The kid sighed. Kate said later if the kid had said "whom" she'd have thrown her out. "But Jasper meant, means, an awful lot to me." And she began to cry, the tears falling from her eyes as of their own accord. She raised her glasses and wiped her eyes on her other sleeve.

"What kind of dog was he?" Kate asked for something to say. "I gather not a mastiff if someone could carry him out."

"He was, is, a Jack Russell terrier. The breed isn't yet accepted by the American Kennel Club, though it is by the

English. Jack Russell terriers are small, very low to the ground, white with brown faces and ears, and tough as anything. Don't you see, it had to be someone Jasper knew, someone he thought was taking him out. He loves to go out," she added, sniffing, "but he's a fierce watchdog with anyone he doesn't know."

"You haven't told me *your* name," Kate said.

"Arabella. It was my father's mother's name. She was a suffragette who chained herself to fences. My father hated her. People like my sister call me Arrie."

Of course it occurred to Kate that the kid needed a therapist, not a detective, and she also probably needed a new father and a new dog. "What about your mother?" she asked. "You haven't mentioned her."

"She's away trying to stop drinking. She's much younger than my father. She was a graduate student. She's his second wife. Roxanna and I have two much older stepsisters from his first marriage. My father has never been able to produce a son, to his sorrow. I hope my mother gets better. The man where she is says the whole family ought to help, but my father hasn't the time. My sister and I went down there once. . . ." She trailed off.

Poor Kate didn't really know what to do. She wanted to help the kid, but there didn't seem to be any evident practical course of assistance. Arrie seemed to understand her dilemma. "You could think about it," she said. "My sister says you're very good at thinking about things. Only try not to think too long because I'm very worried about poor Jasper. He can be very trying to people who don't understand him."

"And with that," Kate said, relating the whole scene to Reed over her second martini, her first having been required simply to calm her down and stop her babbling, "the kid left with a lot more dignity than I was exhibiting. What the hell am I to do? Could you call some old pal from the DA's office to undertake a dog search on the side?"

Kate's husband answered her real question. "The doorman saw someone leave with the dog under his arm, as I understand it. The dog wasn't struggling, indicating that it wasn't being nabbed by a stranger, but by someone it knew. You better find out more about the family."

"It doesn't sound like a family I want to know much more about. Perhaps we should offer to adopt Arrie and get her another Jasper."

"You have got to begin drinking less," Reed said with asperity. "We are a happy, adult couple, let me remind you; you have no trouble remembering it when you're sober. You aren't going to turn maternal on me after all these years?"

"Fear not. Just wait till *you* meet Arrie, not to mention her father, the esteemed Professor Witherspoon."

"What is he a professor of, exactly?"

"Exactly is the word. He deals in manuscripts, the older the better, and in a foreign tongue. There is nothing about them he doesn't know, to do him justice; the trouble is, he doesn't know anything else. Confront him with an idea, and he turns into a dangerous, oversized porcupine with a very loud voice. He detests every new discipline or theory or concept of teaching, and if he had his way he would never have hired the first woman faculty member. He's done his best to keep our numbers down. Women students, needless to say, are a different matter. He carries on with them in a manner designed to give sexual harassment a bad name. Women students should be grateful to sit at his feet and submit themselves in other suitable poses;

he doesn't want them as colleagues. He is also pompous and leering, but we might as well keep this discussion on an impersonal basis, as is my wont."

"That fills out the picture without getting us anywhere, wouldn't you say?"

"I've *been* saying, ever since I got home. What, dear man, is my next move?"

"Something will occur to you," Reed said with confidence.

The next day, Arrie's sister Roxanna Albright phoned Kate's office for an appointment. With enormous relief, Kate agreed to see her. Roxanna, being beautiful and older, could be counted on not to get to Kate in the same way Arrie had. No doubt they could arrive at a practical conclusion to the whole problem, insofar as it allowed of one. Perhaps it would be best to begin by advertising for Jasper, hanging plaintive signs on lampposts, that kind of thing.

Roxanna, whom Kate had unsuccessfully attempted to call to mind from some years back, exceeded all expectations. She was gorgeous, there was no other word. She must, Kate thought, have undergone some sort of transformation in the intervening years; not to have noticed her would have been like overlooking Garbo.

"I don't know whether to apologize or implore," Roxanna said, when they had both sat down. "Arrie didn't consult me before coming; we'd talked about you once at dinner and I'd expressed my admiration. The fact that you had successfully undertaken some detective commissions was mentioned."

"As well as the opinion that I couldn't find a herd of buffalo in a white field; I know. But does the fact that your father despises me really qualify me to help Arrie? If so, I hope you'll tell me how."

"Oh dear. Tact is something Arrie doesn't so much scorn as ignore."

"I quite agree with her," Kate said. "Tact should never interfere with one's getting at the facts. Your father, for example, lacks not tact, but any concept of what the facts are."

"How well you put it." Roxanna paused as though considering how to go on. "I think the world of Arrie," she said. "Arrie's convinced she's an ugly duckling; I talk of a swan, which in time she will become. Arrie's going to do just fine. But for me, she doesn't get much undemanding affection, or really, any affection at all. Except from Jasper, of course, which is what made this so awful. Jasper is a very responsive dog; he and Arrie have a relationship I can only call passionate. That's why I wanted to come in person to tell you that he's back, and apparently no worse for his strange adventure. We got a note, printed in capitals on plain paper, saying he could be found at five P.M. tied to the gate of the playground at Seventy-second Street and Fifth Avenue. Of course, Arrie was there on the dot, and so was Jasper. I've really only come to thank you for your kindness, not throwing her out, listening to her. It was a horrible three days; even my father's glad the dog's back, and that's saying a good deal. You've been very kind."

"There was no ransom asked, no demand at all?"

"None. My father pointed out to Arrie that if she went ahead of time, as she wanted to do, the kidnapper might see her and not return Jasper. It's the only helpful thing he's said in living memory, so I suppose this whole affair is remarkable for that alone." Roxanna rose. "I know," she said, "that Arrie will write to you and thank you for your sympathy and kindness. I thank you too."

The next day, however, brought not a letter from Arrie,

but Arrie herself. She had waited patiently during Kate's office hour until the last of the students had gone. She had Jasper with her, hidden in a very large sack. She let him out in Kate's office, explaining that she had brought him because she hardly dared leave him alone if she didn't absolutely have to, and because she thought Kate might like to meet him, having been so kind about his disappearance.

Jasper was a bundle of energy, perhaps ten inches high and eighteen inches long; he looked as though he could have taken on with ease anything five times his size. Having dashed about with relief at being out of the sack (necessitated by the university's NO DOGS signs), Jasper sat down at Arrie's feet and looked up at her adoringly. Kate began to feel she was being forced to watch a Disney movie that threatened never to end. Arrie, perhaps sensing this, became very businesslike.

"Jasper and I are not here only to thank you," she said. "We wish to engage your services to find out who took him. Unless I know, you see," she added, "I'll never be able to feel safe in leaving him again. I'm sure you can understand that."

Kate was silent—which wasn't, as she was the first to admit, her usual part in a conversation. She had to recognize a clear reluctance to abandon this child to an additional unknown: her father was clearly as reliable as a lottery, her sister affectionate but hardly able, and certainly not obliged, to provide parental attentions. The dog seemed to be the only steady factor, and Kate understood that Arrie's desire for assurance was certainly justified. How, on the other hand, to provide it?

"I have come with a suggestion," Arrie said, reaching over to stroke Jasper, who sat expectantly—Kate doubted if the dog ever sat any other way—at her side. "My father is relieved that I have Jasper back; so is my sister. I think they would be willing to agree if I invited you to dinner."

"To case the joint?" Kate asked. Dinner with Professor Witherspoon, Roxanna, and Arrie, to name only the minimum cast of characters, struck Kate as likely to be bizarre. Apart from everything else, Witherspoon was the sort of man who, alone with three females, becomes either autocratic or flirtatious, neither of them a mode dear to Kate's heart. On the other hand . . .

Arrie had smiled at Kate's question. "Tomorrow night?" she suggested. "Seven o'clock? I've written down the address and phone number. Jasper and I will be grateful."

Kate nodded. What else was there to do? Not for the first time she thanked the gods–Kate, when not agnostic, was firmly polytheistic–that she had very little to do with children in this life.

AT LEAST ONE of Kate's trepidations about the dinner chez Witherspoon was allayed immediately upon her entrance: there were two men in addition to the Professor. At least that cause of Witherspoon's pontification or spriteliness had been removed. Roxanna introduced a young man, almost as gorgeous in his way as she in hers, named Desmond Elliott: an actor. What possibly else? Kate thought, shaking hands; he was good enough to eat. Arrie she greeted with warmth and a wink; Jasper had been, it appeared, exiled for the duration. The other guest was an older man who, it became immediately clear, was allied with Witherspoon and against the others. Why, Kate wondered, was that so clear? Equally clear, somewhat less inexplicably, was the fact that Mr. Johnson was a lawyer who had joined them for dinner when Arrie's invitation to Kate superseded his planned dinner à deux with Witherspoon. The Professor had decided upon graciousness. He was the host, and while in his house Kate would be treated like a woman guest, neither more nor less. With relief, Kate sank into a chair, accepted a drink, and embarked upon a sea of meaningless chitchat. This torture was somewhat ameliorated by Desmond Elliott's amusing account of the actor's life, made up, it appeared, in equal parts, of being a waiter and performing in small, unprofitable companies of great artistic integrity so far "off" Broadway as to be in another state.

Roxanna was a pleasant hostess, keeping an eye on everyone's comfort, but not buzzing about or insisting upon anything. When they moved in to dinner, she brought things gracefully to the table; she and Desmond were the mainstays of the conversation, although Witherspoon made some acidic comments to Kate about their department which Kate did her best to ignore. It is difficult, while eating your host's meat, to convey to him that you disagree with everything he is saying and everything he is likely to say. They finally reached the blessed subject of the university's administration, in disdain for which even sworn enemies could agree.

As the company returned to the living room for coffee, Arrie asked Kate if she would like to say hello to Jasper. Kate eagerly agreed, and followed Arrie down the hall to a closed door, behind which sharp barks of anticipation could be heard. "Quiet, Jasper," Arrie said, revealing a history of complaints—from whom it was not hard to guess. "Up." The dog danced on his short hind legs, and Arrie took from her pocket a chunk of chicken breast; she tossed it into the air and Jasper caught and swallowed it in one grateful gulp, then sat, hoping for more.

"You have a nice room," Kate said.

"Yes. I used to have a tiny room off the kitchen, but Roxanna took that since she doesn't really live here most of the time. There's really just me and my father now."

"And Jasper," Kate said, it being the only cheerful fact that occurred to her. "Did your father buy him for you?" she added hopefully.

"No. Roxanna did. Dad said I couldn't keep him. But then he changed his mind. Roxanna made him."

"Desmond's nice," Kate observed. It *was* odd how conversation deserted her in the presence of the very young.

"Very nice. I'm glad he was here. I don't care for Mr. Johnson."

"Does he come often?"

"No, he's never really been here before. I've just talked to him on the phone when he calls my father. Roxanna says he's simultaneously illiterate and imperious." Kate tried not to grin, and failed. They laughed together, and Jasper rose to his hind legs, joining in.

"I still need to know who took him," Arrie said before they rejoined the others.

REED HAD PROMISED that something would occur to Kate, but all that occurred to her was gossip. And for departmental gossip, the ultimate source was Richard Frankel. Dean Rosovsky, when he became semiretired from his high post at Harvard, reported in the Harvard magazine that the first duty of a dean was to listen to gossip. Kate, not to be outdone by any dean, took the advice to heart. Richard, reached by telephone, was graciously pleased to make an appointment the following day for lunch.

Kate contemplated his face across the luncheon table

with pleasure. Richard combined the best features of an imp and a youthfully aging and gay (in all senses of the word) uncle. He was, in fact, quite heterosexual and a confirmed bachelor, having convinced everyone of this except himself. He still hoped to meet the right woman in the next day or so, and launch himself on a satisfactory career of marriage and fatherhood. Like a number of people Kate had observed over the years, Richard, marvelously suited to his life and vigorously happy, was unaware that his deep satisfaction arose in part from the delusion that he was abjectly in need of passionate love, babies, and a deep and lasting relationship. Kate liked him enormously.

She did not immediately ask about Witherspoon. To have evinced that much interest would have started Richard's investigative motors, and Kate did not wish to reveal her relationship with Arrie. But it was easy to work the conversation around to Witherspoon, whom Richard, together with the greater part of the department, despised with a vigor mitigated only by the pleasure they got in talking about how bloody awful he was. Witherspoon, Kate was forced to realize, had provided a good deal of pleasure in his curmudgeonly life, none of it intended.

Richard knew all about the wife, tucked away in a nearer version of Betty Ford's detoxification facility. "Before my time of course, but the usual story. He pursued her with tales of his unsympathetic wife; now she's the unsympathetic wife: they never learn, poor dears. One hopes the graduate students these days are too smart to marry him, if not quite smart enough to dodge him entirely. I met the wife once; he had me to dinner in the early days, before I turned out to be too modern altogether. Obviously a lady, and punishing him and herself for her stupid mistake. They have two daughters, an absolutely mouthwatering

creature called Roxanna, and an afterthought called Arabella. The names are enough to give you an idea of the
marriage. It's widely assumed that Arabella isn't his
child."

Kate stared at him. "On what grounds?" she finally
asked.

"I think it was the poor thing's final attempt to bolt,
before she drowned herself in alcohol reinforced by prescription drugs. Considering his record of fornication and
adultery, you'd think he'd have turned a blind eye, but not
our Witherspoon."

"Why not?"

"Kate, my sweet, you don't seem your usual quick-witted
self, if you'll forgive my observing it. Must you go on
grunting monosyllabic questions?"

"I'm sorry, Richard. I'm always astonished at how much
life is like prime-time soap operas."

"Which I'm certain you never watch. They are unreal
only in the way outrageous situations follow hard upon
each other, if not occurring simultaneously, and in the
luxury of the surroundings. Actually, they are, otherwise,
just like life, if you're a shit like Witherspoon, which of
course most of the characters are. Have you some special
interest in him? A renewed fascination with manuscripts?"

Kate laughed. "If I could take the smallest interest in
manuscripts, it wouldn't be renewed. It would be a new
and sudden aberration. Actually, I had dinner there the
other evening, and was overwhelmed with curiosity. Roxanna used to be a student of mine, and she asked me."
Richard would wonder why she hadn't mentioned this in
the first place; the reason was clear to Kate: it had entailed
lying.

"Ah. I wondered why your interest was so suddenly

awakened. The rumor is that he now wants a divorce and most of what there is of her worldly goods. In exchange, he'll pretend to relinquish with infinite sorrow custody of Arabella."

"Do you mean he'll get her to pay him alimony?"

"Don't ask me the details, but that's often how it works out these days. The woman gets the children and the man gets the property."

"Surely the woman gets to keep what she brought into the marriage."

"No doubt," Richard dryly said. "But since all this wife brought in was her misguided affection for Witherspoon, that's unlikely to serve her very well. Of course, she may have some family bonds stashed away, in which case he'll do his best to get them. The men can always afford the better lawyers, alas."

"No doubt the men look at it differently," Kate said, her mind elsewhere.

"We certainly can guess how Witherspoon looks at it. And he's got two daughters from the former marriage, both unlikely to have great sympathy with the poor alcoholic. Maybe Roxanna and Arabella will come to her defense. I had the most awful row with him, you know, not too long ago. That's why it's an additional pleasure to contemplate his absolute awfulness. He worked every angle to get tenure for one of his acolytes, a twerp with his nose in manuscripts and his brain in a sling. A born ass-licker and fool. Witherspoon got his way, of course, and I was marked down as an enemy, a mark not of distinction, since there are so many of us, but of honor. The only good part of the story is that the twerp left to devote himself wholly to some manuscript collection. Did Witherspoon behave himself at dinner?"

"Oh yes. The older daughter is very gracious, and I like

the younger one. I'm surprised the wife had the gumption to have a love affair."

"Its end was no doubt the inevitable last straw. Witherspoon made no bones about the fact that if the child had been a boy he would have forgiven everything. He's that kind of monster."

"Do you think he's really the father?"

"God knows. Roxanna is pretty definitely his, and she's gorgeous, so who has an opinion about genes? Of course, the wife was pretty luscious in those days; he'd never have bothered otherwise, that being all women are good for."

"Do you know anything about the lover? He sounds mysterious, like the tutor who might have been Edith Wharton's father."

"I know the scuttlebutt: he was thin, with glasses and buckteeth, and very sweet. He was an adjunct teacher in art history, which she dabbled in. I don't know what became of him; gossip has it they used to walk around the campus holding hands. I feel sorry for her."

Kate was amazed, not for the first time, at the extent of her colleagues' interest in one another's lives. Richard was, of course, unofficial keeper of the gossip; since his heart was always in the right place, she was willing to decide that his was a valuable function. What Witherspoon would have thought of it was another question. Did she care what Witherspoon thought about anything, or only what he did?

What had he done, apart from being a failure as a human being and a father? Kate decided to walk for a while, after bidding Richard a grateful farewell. She wandered around the city streets, noticing dogs (no Jack Russell terriers) and the general air of menace which by now everyone in New York, and probably elsewhere, took for granted: it seemed the mark of an age. Compared to which, Kate told herself, the momentary absence of a dog was hardly to be counted.

And yet, there had been, somewhere along the family chain, a failure of trust, which was how menace began. Was it Kant who had said that trust was the basis of civilization? Letting her attention wander unbidden over the cast of characters at that dinner, and in Richard's account of the Witherspoons, Kate found herself eventually at Central Park at Seventy-second Street; she sat on a bench to observe the spot where Jasper had been tied when Arrie retrieved him. It was a well-chosen location, easily approached and abandoned from four directions, sufficiently crowded with people and dogs entering and leaving the park to make one more man and dog unnoticed. Man? A man had removed Jasper from the building, according to the doorman's report. Dogs were not allowed in the playground, so a number of them were tied to the entrance, waiting, with accustomed patience or anxiety, for their people on the other side of the fence. By the time Kate had to leave to meet her class, she had made up her mind.

"IT IS, OF course, none of my business," Kate said to Roxanna, as they had a drink before ordering their dinner. "That phrase is always a sign that someone thinks it is her business, or has determined to make it so. Do you mind?"

"Hardly," Roxanna said. "I used to wonder what it would be like to have dinner with Professor Fansler. Thank you for the privilege: my business is your business."

"Very graciously put. Perhaps you had better order another drink."

"Oh dear," Roxanna said.

"I intend nothing more sinister than blackmail," Kate said reassuringly.

"I know: on behalf of Arrie. Blackmail will not be necessary. From you, that is; I've already employed it on her behalf. Is that what you guessed?"

"It would hardly be fair to get you to tell me what happened, and then claim to have guessed it all."

"Okay," Roxanna said. "You tell me. And I'll take that second drink. May I correct you as you go along?"

"Please do," Kate said. "My hope is that you will end up assuring me about poor Jasper's safety."

Roxanna nodded.

"Your father, the revered Professor Witherspoon, has been after what money he can get out of your mother. Doubtless he has another young lady in tow. I say 'lady,' because I don't really think a *woman* would have anything to do with him. Did he try to retrieve from your mother something he had given her and now wanted to give to another? A ring, a brooch—it can't have been too big, or Jasper wouldn't have swallowed it, however imbedded in a piece of meat. Although the way he gulps, dancing around on his hind legs, anything is possible."

"Not a ring," Roxanna said. "An emerald. He had had it taken out of the ring. He said he was going to get it reset. It's the most valuable thing my mother had. It was in her family for years; they may have pawned it, but they never sold it."

"He pretended to her it needed to be reset?"

"Nothing so civilized. She would have been suspicious immediately at any kindly offer, I'm afraid. He talked her out of taking it to the detoxification place, said it might be stolen. She didn't believe him, but when he set his mind on something, she didn't have a chance. I heard them arguing about it one night. So did Desmond, the guy you met; he was there with me. He held me back from interfering; he was right."

"He's very handsome, even for an actor," Kate said.

"He's especially handsome for a lawyer, which is what he is," Roxanna responded. "We were trying to allay my father's suspicions. He knew we'd overheard him. So when he emerged that evening, we pretended innocence, on Desmond's advice, and I introduced him to Dad as an actor. His looks, as you observed, made that easy."

"I've lost count," Kate said, "but I don't think I'm doing too well. Shall we order dinner?"

"The details need cleaning up, but you certainly seem to be onto the main story line. Go on."

"There isn't much more. Somehow, later, needing to hide the stolen emerald, the Professor fed it to Jasper. Anyone who observed Jasper's routine with Arrie would have thought of it, whether the motive was greed or detection. Was he going to kill the dog?"

"Of course. Or pay someone else to. Fortunately, I guessed what he was up to. I had caught him examining the stone. I demanded it and he wouldn't give it to me. Sometime later, he came in to promise me he wouldn't take it out of the house. There was something about the exact way he said this that made me suspicious. I pretended to calm down and then went to look for the stone; it wasn't where it was supposed to be. My father went into calm assurances that he didn't have it, and hadn't hid it, urging me to search him. He was so smug about it all; that, and the sight of Jasper dancing around gave me the idea. He had fed it to the dog in a hunk of meat, intending to have the dog 'get lost.' When I figured this out we really had a knockdown fight. I couldn't believe he'd really do that to Arrie."

"Where was Arrie?"

"Locked in the bathroom, crying. She hated the fights.

She used to stuff her ears with toilet paper. He and I fought about a lot of things, though never as violently as this. In the end, I threatened him. You see, my mother had mentioned her ring when Arrie and I went to see her; she wanted Arrie to have it. Arrie said I should have it because I was beautiful. My mother hugged Arrie and said: 'You take care of Roxanna; it's far, far better not to be beautiful, believe me, my darling.' "

"And you got Desmond to leave with the dog under his arm. I gather Jasper had got to know him by now."

"Jasper takes a long time to get to know people well enough to let them pick him up. He may be small, but he's tough. That was me."

"In drag?"

"Great fun. I got the idea from Sherlock Holmes. 'My walking clothes,' Irene Adler called them. Desmond borrowed the suit for me from someone my size. I can't remember when I had more fun. The doorman didn't raise an eyebrow."

"So you took Jasper—where?"

"To Desmond's, where I stay most of the time. I walked him, and never have I used a pooper-scooper more diligently. At first, we thought we'd keep him in, but poor Jasper is well trained. I tell you, retrieving that emerald from Jasper's shit made me feel like someone in a Dickens novel, *Our Mutual Friend* for choice. I well remember your talking about that novel."

"You said you'd get the emerald back if he behaved?"

"More than behaved. I had Desmond as a witness and advisor. I said Arrie and Jasper were to live with me, that he was to give my mother a divorce under fair terms: he could keep the apartment, he had to continue to support Arrie till she finished her education, my mother was to get half his pension, and if he didn't agree I was going to drag him into court accused of theft and abusive conduct."

"And he bought it?"

"Not entirely. I had to give him the emerald, and a few other things besides. But I figured I didn't need it, Arrie didn't need it, it hadn't done my mother much good, and it was worth her freedom and ours. I also told him I had a student lined up ready to bring charges of sexual harassment. I scared him. He even cooperated about Arrie's retrieving Jasper. I was going to make him leave the dog at the playground, but I didn't want him to take out his frustrations on the poor beast. So I did that too. Desmond came with me between two closings. Desmond's been great."

"He sounds rather unusual for a lawyer."

"He is. He's quitting. He says there's no point spending your life suing about water damage and helping one firm take over another. I don't know what he's going to do."

"You might suggest acting," Kate said. "And being a waiter on the side."

"He's thinking of becoming a detective," Roxanna said. "A private eye. Perhaps he could get in touch with you for pointers."

Kate decided not to look for irony in this. "What next?" she asked.

"It's Arrie's vacation next week. We're going down with Desmond to visit my mom. I think with some real encouragement, and the knowledge that the Professor is out of her life, she may actually make it. She never took up drinking, or prescription drugs either, till she met him. But she's going to need a lot of help."

"Speaking of 'none of my business,' " Kate said, "may I ask an outrageous question? Just tell me to go to hell if you don't want to answer it. Is the Professor Arrie's father, or was there someone else?"

"I'll answer that question on one condition," Roxanna said. "That you agree to do me an enormous favor, no questions asked. Is it a bargain?"

"I'll have to think about it," Kate said. "I don't believe in blind promises."

"And I don't believe in gossip, not all of it. My mother did moon around with another guy. His main attraction was that he wasn't lustful. My father is very lustful. He insisted on his rights; that's how he thought of them, as rights. And he still wanted a son."

"You've been angry at him a long time, haven't you?" Kate said.

"I'm getting over it, with help. I don't want Arrie to go through the same thing. Of course, I couldn't have done it without Desmond, especially since the Professor had that sleazy lawyer on his side. Mr. Johnson: you met him too."

Kate looked into her coffee cup. "All right," she said. "It's a bargain."

Roxanna looked up questioningly.

"I'll keep Jasper for Arrie while she's gone. Reed will be overjoyed. That is, I'll pretend we have him forever, and when he finds out it's only a week or so, he'll be overjoyed."

"I think women are reprehensible," Roxanna said. "Don't you?" And they laughed together. Kate even found herself wishing Arrie and Jasper had been there.

THE DISAPPEARANCE OF

GREAT AUNT FLAVIA

Great Aunt Flavia was the only member of the older generation of Kate Fansler's family to whom Kate would give the time of day. "Even a minute is too precious to waste on Fanslers," she used to say. "Some people spend time with other people just because they're family, but I spend time only with those who move me forward into experience, not backward into memory or resentment or weary tolerance."

"You've got it down pat," I said. "You must have rehearsed it. You better watch out or you'll start sounding pompous."

" 'Authoritative' is the word you want. 'Bossy' if you insist, but not, I beg you, Leighton, 'pompous.' As you will realize before long," Kate said, "when you decide to have nothing to do with your family, you have to have the reasons down pat; you have to live with them safely accepted by your unconscious. Otherwise, you're more in family company than if you saw your family weekly. How did we get on that dreary subject?"

"It's Great Aunt Flavia," I said. Kate sometimes calls her Great Aunt Flavia because my cousin Leo and I do. Otherwise she just calls her Flavia, and with great affection. Great Aunt Flavia is, properly speaking, neither an aunt nor a Fansler except by marriage (his second) to one of Kate's uncles. The Fanslers were, until Kate came along, unremittingly masculine. Kate has three much older brothers; Kate's father had three brothers. One of these, left a widower, married the much younger Flavia–who, Kate conjectured, had tired of chastity and decided to try another mode. She had produced, at the latest possible moment, a son, and as her husband slipped into senility she embraced eccentricity or what the Fanslers called plain dottiness. Leo and I tended to find Great Aunt Flavia a bit much until Kate told us to see Lily Tomlin as a bag lady in touch with people from outer space. "Great Aunt Flavia to a T," Kate said, "in spirit if not literal fact. She has too much money to be a bag lady, but I'm sure she comes as close as her income allows." The Fanslers are very rich and very dull; Kate thought it to Great Aunt Flavia's eternal credit that becoming, as a Fansler, the first had not entailed becoming, like a Fansler, the second.

"What's happened to Great Aunt Flavia?" Kate asked.

"The family fears she intends to kill herself," I said. "They thought you might rally round." Kate's family does not usually call upon her for assistance of any sort; doubtless they felt, in this case, that one prodigal could help another.

"How characteristic of them," Kate said. "They have considered her nothing but a nuisance and a burden, but when she decides to take control of her life, they interfere because she isn't playing by their rule book. Flavia is seventy-five if she's a day; she ought to know whether she wants to live or not. Why in the world did she confide in them about her plans?"

"She didn't. She made the mistake of consulting her lawyer about bequests and such. He sneaked to one of your brothers, or maybe a wife. Great Aunt Flavia is furious."

"As well she might be. Can't she just tell them to buzz off?"

"Of course. But Daddy, knowing I like you or, as he puts it, allow you undue influence over me, thought I might talk you into talking Great Aunt Flavia out of doing anything drastic. Between us, I don't know if he's worried about her or her money; most of it's in trust for the son, of course, but Great Aunt Flavia has a good bit of her own, and under Fansler surveillance it has grown and ought not to be allowed to wander off unattended. To do them justice, they may even be feeling a pang of guilt: they've never really treated Great Aunt Flavia well. Anyway, it was thought that you would sneer at Daddy but listen to me. You have to give him credit for that much intelligence."

"Are you suggesting that I call up Great Aunt Flavia and ask her intentions, counseling caution?"

"Something like that."

"Well," Kate said, "I may call her; I was about to anyway. But I don't promise a thing. Not a thing. And you can tell that to your daddy." Kate dislikes all her brothers, but my father most of all, since he is the youngest and should know better.

"THANK YOU, DEAR," Flavia said. "You do know how to give one a proper tea unlaced with nostalgia. Do you think we might move on to something a bit more fortified?" Kate, grinning, offered her a Scotch and soda, taking one herself. They were used to toasting each other. "None better, damn few as good," Great Aunt Flavia liked to say, not just repeating herself, but admitting a tradition and an alliance.

"They've put you onto me, haven't they?" Flavia, once fortified, asked.

"Yes," Kate said. "But I refused. It did remind me, though, that I'd been missing you. One of the defects of liking the young is that one is always the oldest person in the room. You make a welcome change."

"I know what you mean. And that's especially hard for the likes of you and me who grew up used to being the youngest. Have you ever seen a movie called *It's a Wonderful Life*–James Stewart at Christmas?"

"Not that I can remember," Kate said. "Have you taken to watching old movies?"

"I've taken to watching television. Gives you an idea of what's going on, what people believe in. I think it's frightful, but I can't keep myself from watching."

Kate was delighted. Great Aunt Flavia had never even owned a television set. She, Kate, did not watch much television, but she hoped, at Flavia's age, to become more open-minded. It was vital to acquire new habits in old age, boldly countering old prejudices, Kate said.

"In this movie," Flavia explained, "James Stewart plays a man who decides to jump into the river. The reasons aren't important, except that he considers his life a failure. He isn't old enough for such a decision, of course, he has little children, but no one who doesn't play a villain or a doctor can be old in movies. Things only happen to the young, even inappropriate things. One has to overlook it, in the name of sex. Anyway, he is rescued by an angel."

"An angel?" Kate asked.

"Yes. He's male and timid and not quite successful, and he sets out to prove to James Stewart how much poorer everyone would be had he never lived. We learn that his wife without him would have become a spinster in glasses working in a library (a fate of hideous proportions, needless to say, despite the fact that she is played by a gorgeous actress who would have had no trouble joining a well-paying high-class bordello), that some druggist would have killed someone with the wrong prescription, that the bad man, Lionel Barrymore (who *is* allowed to be old), would have taken over the town—you get the picture."

"It's clear enough," Kate said, "and sounds a very good reason not to watch television."

"Well, it was originally a movie, but they show it every Christmas. I've studied it carefully, and have decided that it is garbage in at least three different ways, but what really struck home, *despite* the movie, was the simple truth that because you've mattered in life doesn't mean you can go on mattering. James Stewart has friends who pay his bills, and little children, and a luscious spouse, but his past—anyone's past—is hardly the point. It's what you have now that makes you decide whether or not to jump into the river in winter, figuratively speaking."

"I quite agree," Kate said. "There is only the present."

"Thank God," Flavia said, holding out her glass. "Someone who understands."

"Which is not to say," Kate said, handing it back to her refilled, "that I necessarily agree with your view of your present. I might agree, but I need to be persuaded. Try me."

"I started talking to people about giving away my money, for scholarships, guaranteeing college to poor children who finish high school, that sort of thing. I soon discovered that while I was eagerly courted by those in charge of scholarships and such, it was my money they wanted; I was just a means of getting it, I didn't matter. I know I can trust you not to deny so obvious an observation."

"You can. But there's always the matter of deciding where to give it. Only you can do that."

"I have. Spent quite a time at it. I can leave all my money."

"And then not have any more to live on?"

"Not even that. The income from the trust fund that is mine for life and then will go to Martin is more than ample. More than ample."

"Yes," Kate said. "I see."

"You're such a comfort to me, dear," Flavia said. "You see things."

"I can't help feeling all the same that you haven't taken advantage of your age and station in life."

"Meaning?"

"Meaning you have enough money and are invisible. Have you thought where that could lead?"

"Invisible?" Flavia looked at her hand as though expecting to find it gone.

"I mean, when a woman is old, no one sees her unless she comes attached to money or some other sort of power that brings her momentarily into focus. So you must hold on to your money to become visible when you choose. It will, all in good time, get to the right causes. Meanwhile, why not have on your magic cap, be invisible, discover things?"

"I see what you mean." Like Kate and me and my cousin Leo but like no other Fanslers, Great Aunt Flavia can leap from insight to insight, passing over the connections between. "You mean like Agatha Christie's Miss Marple—pussyfoot around. Notice people when they don't notice you. See what's going on. Be clever."

"Exactly," Kate said. "Too few people take advantage of the fun of being old; they're always trying to pass for young."

"I'll have another watercress sandwich," Flavia said. "It's

almost dinnertime; this will save me having to think about eating." She already had a faraway look in her eye.

SOME CONSIDERABLE TIME LATER, I had to tell Kate that the family was again worried about Great Aunt Flavia. "Worried" was a nice word in the circumstances; they were hysterical.

"It's Great Aunt Flavia," I said when I had got Kate on the phone. "She's disappeared."

"Disappeared!" Kate all but shouted.

"In the South," I said.

"The South," Kate said, softer this time. I really was annoyed with her.

"If you're just going to keep repeating everything I say, it will not help Flavia."

"I suppose she was visiting Georgiana," Kate said.

"You guessed right. Georgiana was quite upset on the telephone, I understand. She called Larry, you not being available." Larry is Kate's brother, not my father, probably the stuffiest of the brothers, which is a little like saying that one elephant is bigger than another.

"When did Flavia disappear?"

"Several days ago. Georgiana, being Southern, wanted to wait awhile before causing a fuss."

"What was she waiting for?" Kate shouted, but I had already decided to hang up and go see Kate in person. She tended to repeat herself more on the phone than when face to face. I knew she would call Georgiana, and I wanted to be with Kate when she decided what to do, to keep informed and be part of the action. Kate never means to overlook me, but she tends to get involved and forget to tell me things.

Georgiana Montgomery had been to Bryn Mawr with

Flavia at a time when few women went to college—so Great Aunt Flavia always told us—and nice young ladies from the South never went to college, and certainly never to a Northern college. But Georgiana's mother, who was from the North, expected her daughter to do great things, to challenge Southern ladyhood. So much for parental expectations: the nearest Georgiana came in her youth to challenging anything was in befriending Flavia. They were freshman roommates by college fiat, and roommates after that by choice. Georgiana returned South after graduation and married a proper Southern gentleman, who died twenty years later leaving her a childless and (one supposed) rich widow. All Georgiana would ever tell Flavia was that she was "comfortable."

But Great Aunt Flavia must have had more of an effect on Georgiana than anyone realized, because bit by bit Georgiana began to work for civil rights for blacks (who, Flavia said, were called colored people in those days), and by civil rights Georgiana meant the whole bag: votes, education, desegregation all along the line. Georgiana kept her local friends because she was from an important family, had married into an important family, and was a fine person, and because (Kate guessed) she stuck to civil rights, and never went in for any other fancy ideas, like the Equal Rights Amendment, or sexual liberation, or divorce, or the idea that man's lot wasn't just as hard as woman's. She wanted the colored people to have their fair rights, and apart from that, she led the life of a Southern lady.

Flavia visited Georgiana for a month every spring, both before Flavia's husband died and after. Flavia used to say life took on a new prospect in the South, where one lived in an orderly, gracious fashion, inhaling the scent of magnolias or verbena or whatever they grow in the South, having lemonade on the porch, paying calls on

Georgiana's friends and having them to dinner. Most of the civil rights business was done by Georgiana on the telephone, and intruded little into their daily routine. They went their separate ways in the morning, had their lunch, separately or together in one of the nice restaurants in town (Georgiana said preparing lunch was just too much for her housekeeper), and met in the late afternoon for tea or, more likely, lemonade. Flavia said it was a most relaxing life, for one month a year.

By the time I got to Kate's, she had reached Georgiana on the telephone and was obviously listening to some long explanation; she motioned me to sit down and keep quiet. Unobserved I would have picked up an extension and listened in, but Kate thought eavesdropping on telephone calls on the order of poisoning wells (it poisoned trust), so I waited for her to hang up and start telling me what was going on.

As it turned out, there wasn't much to tell. The last time Georgiana saw Flavia, they had had dinner with some friends, and sat around together for a while talking of this and that. Then Flavia and Georgiana had gone to bed. A perfectly ordinary evening. Georgiana always breakfasted in her room and stayed there throughout the morning attending to business. Flavia had breakfast in the breakfast room—nothing in the least unusual. When Georgiana came downstairs preparatory to going out to lunch, she learned that Flavia had already left for her own luncheon engagement. From which Flavia never returned.

"That's the last anybody heard from her?" I asked. "How many days ago?"

"Three days ago, four if we count today," Kate said. "Georgiana heard from Flavia once, on the evening of the day she didn't return. She sounded rather breathless, and simply said: 'Don't worry about me if you don't see me for a

while. I'm just away for a few days. I can't call because
they'll probably listen in on your telephone. Don't worry.'
Georgiana insists that was the whole and exact message, and
I've never seen any reason to doubt what Georgiana says."

"What are you going to do?" I asked Kate.

"I'm going there, of course," Kate said. "I have a horrible feeling I'm responsible for all this." I knew Kate
wouldn't let me come, and she didn't, but she did promise
to call me every evening from a phone booth, in case
Georgiana's telephone was tapped.

"You're kidding," I said.

"Leighton," Kate said sternly, while throwing things into
a flight bag (Kate is not one of your neat packers), "if you
don't think we live in a total surveillance society, you had
better wake up. Have you any idea the watch that can be
kept on people?" she added darkly. "Please try to be home
each day at six in the evening." And with that she was gone.

KATE WENT RIGHT to Georgiana's from the airport and
heard the whole story again while drinking lemonade on
the porch. Georgiana said she had informed the police
about Flavia's disappearance, and they had made all the
usual inquiries–the morgue, hospitals, reports of vagrants,
old ladies hanging around bus and train stations or air-
ports–all to no avail. "No avail," Georgiana repeated,
sighing. She had always feared Flavia would do something
impulsive and foolish, and clearly Flavia had gone and
done it.

"Was there anything unusual about her this time?" Kate
asked Georgiana. "Was she noticeably different than on
her previous visits?"

"Yes and no," Georgiana said, in her slow, Southern
way. Kate had long ago discovered that Southerners do not

think as slowly as they talk, but Northerners have to train themselves not to snatch the ends of sentences out of the mouths of their Southern friends. "Flavia seemed more, you might say *purposeful*, than I remembered her. She asked more questions, and read the papers more intensely. She even seemed more interested in my Merryfields day. Before, she always refused to go with me, saying she saw enough old folks without looking for them."

"Merryfields?" Kate asked.

"The old people's home, nursing home really, but we don't like to call it that. For old folks who can't care for themselves anymore, and haven't any family hereabouts. It's a nice place, for a place like that. Not like the nursing homes I read about in New York."

Kate merely nodded. The last thing she wanted at the moment was to get Georgiana started on the merits of the South and the horrors of New York, not what Kate thought of as a productive conversation at the best of times. "Flavia seemed more interested in–er–Merryfields this time?"

"Much more interested. She surprised me right at first by offering to come with me for my weekly visit when I hadn't even asked her–she'd always refused and I thought the question of her coming was moot. Then she asked all sorts of questions about it, and talked to many of the women patients. There are many more women patients than men, as you might expect. She even wanted to stay on when I was ready to go. I was quite concerned. 'You aren't thinking you might end up in a place like that, I hope, Flavia,' I said, 'because I wouldn't allow it. You'd make your home right here with me,' I said."

"And what did she say to that?" Kate asked when Georgiana's pause was longer than could be accounted for by the speech habits of the South.

"She said: 'You're a dear, Georgiana, and you know there's always a place for you in New York with me, if the situations should be reversed.' Now that's about as likely as a blizzard in Alabama, but I appreciated the thought. Anyway, she wasn't looking at Merryfields in a personal way, so I paid the matter no more mind. When Flavia's here she always goes her own way until teatime, and I was glad she seemed occupied and busy. Mostly when she visits she reads a whole lot, but this time she seemed to spend hours in the town noticing things. I took that as a good sign; lack of interest is bad in the old. I was glad not to have to worry about Flavia on that score. I couldn't have known, could I, that she would disappear and worry me just when I was easy in my mind?"

Kate nodded her understanding of Georgiana's worry.

"Do you think I ought to consult the family lawyer, Matthew Finley?" Georgiana asked Kate after a time. "He's the son of our old family lawyer, and his granddaddy was Papa's lawyer before that. He's young, but he understands how to deal with the world and with old folks like me. Maybe he could give us some good advice."

"We ought to keep him in reserve, anyway," Kate said. "In case we actually have some facts to deal with. Meantime, I think I'll just poke around a little on my own. Try not to worry too much; the old saw about no news being good news was invented for situations just like this. Besides, I can't imagine Flavia doing anything foolish, not really."

"That's the difference between us," Georgiana said. "I can."

KATE STAYED SEVERAL days with Georgiana, hoping for a sign from Great Aunt Flavia, but there wasn't the breath of a sign. Kate called me each day at six from a phone booth as she had promised, but she had nothing to report. The police, egged on by Georgiana's influential friends and relations, had stepped up their search, but they'd found nothing. Kate was ready to retreat back to the North, since there seemed little anyone could do down there among the magnolias or verbena or whatever it is, when the most extraordinary story appeared in the papers with the sudden force of a powerful explosion. The minister of one of the most successful of the fundamentalist churches, who had collected millions of dollars in the service of God at His explicit direction, was photographed entering a motel in Georgiana's town with a prostitute. There was no question of the woman's profession, nor of her understanding of her client's intentions as they entered the motel. By that evening, the minister himself was on television—most of his congregation were reached in this way—pleading for forgiveness of his sin and promising to reform. Kate, for reasons she could not explain to herself let alone to Georgiana, decided to stay on for a bit.

When she called me that evening, she said she was talking from Georgiana's phone, since there wasn't any more anyone could learn by listening in. At Kate's insistence, Georgiana had called Matthew Finley, the family lawyer, and urged him in her gentle but firm manner to discover from the newspaper that had first printed the picture where they had got it. Georgiana told Finley she would wait by her phone for an answer, but could not give a reason. She made it clear, however, that her future legal business depended on prompt action: this disappearance of Flavia had gone on long enough, and if Kate thought this information would hasten Flavia's return, she, Georgiana, would supply it.

Finley stopped asking questions and went to work. He

rang back with the information in a remarkably short time. Kate, listening to Georgiana receive it on the telephone, fought the impulse to grab the receiver from Georgiana's gentle hands.

"I don't know what you expected, my dear," Georgiana said when she had hung up after thanking Finley in her deliberate way, "but the photograph was dropped off at the paper anonymously; that is, it was left at the reception desk, and no one remembers who left it. It was marked 'urgent,' but bore no message other than the name of the minister in the picture."

"An invisible person left it," Kate announced. "Didn't they check out the picture?"

"I was just coming to that, dear," Georgiana mildly said, while Kate wondered if stressful impatience could shorten one's life by decades, as seemed likely. "The newspaper sent out an 'investigative reporter,'" Georgiana ever so lightly emphasized the phrase, "and he found the–er– woman in the picture. She admitted readily enough that it was indeed she, and that the man with her was indeed the minister, whose photograph the reporter showed her. She had not known who her 'client' was, but this was not the first time she had 'serviced' him. Poor Matthew Finley was quite embarrassed at having to report this unseemly business. When they had verified all this, the newspaper people decided to print the picture."

"The rest is history," Kate said. "Georgiana, may I stay on a day or two more? I think I may be able to find Flavia. But I'm going to have to visit your old people's home, Merryland, as soon as possible."

"Merryfields, dear. We'll go this very minute, if you'll just let me get ready. Surely you don't think one of those old people did Flavia in?"

"I think they did the naughty minister in," Kate said. "But only time will tell."

"If you want any information from the old people, Kate," Georgiana said, pausing on the staircase, "perhaps you had better let me try to elicit it. Your rather, well, *Northern* manner might just confuse them, and take more time in the end. Besides, they know me. Now what is it you're trying to discover?" Kate, who could not but see the force of Georgiana's words, had to consent, but she wondered if she would survive waiting for Georgiana to return with her information. I told Kate later that now, at last, she knew how *I* felt when she left me so cruelly suspended in the course of investigations.

Georgiana allowed Kate to go with her to Merryfields, but not to accompany her upstairs on her visits to the old people. "You'll just upset them; even if you don't speak (and we know how unlikely that is, dear), just the presence of a stranger may very well put them off their stride. Now you just sit in the waiting room and *wait.*" No one but Georgiana could have got away with it.

But when she came down again a considerable time later, it was clear that she thought she had got what Kate wanted. And Kate, when she heard it, thought so too. "Though what this has to do with Flavia's disappearance, I cannot imagine," Georgiana announced in the face of Kate's excitement.

Georgiana reported that the dear old ladies had told her *all* about the visits of her dear friend from the North: Flavia. They tended to wander and to repeat themselves, but there was no doubt the conversation had certainly turned to the Divine Church of the Air, which they watched assiduously. Surely, they told Flavia, their dear Minister was talking to each of them personally, because he had read their letters, had answered them personally, and was grateful that their contributions, slight as they were, were helping to spread the word of God and lead others to be born again to Christ. Each lady had shown Flavia her letters, typed of course but addressed to her personally, with the minister's promise to pray for her with special fervor and by name. Each old person, however deserted in this world, was not forgotten by God or by His minister on earth and the Divine Church of the Air. The ladies had even trusted Georgiana with a few of their letters, which Georgiana produced.

"How much money did they send?" Kate asked. Of course Georgiana didn't like to ask the *exact* amount, but it had been as much as the poor dears could afford. They didn't have much left over after paying for their care: just a little for personal use, most of which they were honored to give to the dear Minister.

"Flavia must have felt like throwing up," Kate said without thinking. Georgiana, firm in her breeding, ignored this. Kate saw her into her car, and left, saying she would return soon, and assuring Georgiana that Flavia too would soon be back.

"BUT HOW DID you know where to look?" I asked Kate when she had returned to New York, bringing Flavia with her. Flavia had thought she owed it to Georgiana to stay on a few days, but Kate wouldn't hear of it. "You can never be as invisible as all that, not in Georgiana's house," Kate said, and to this they all had to agree.

"I began with camera stores," Kate said. "Flavia hadn't taken a camera down with her, so she had to have acquired one. Oddly enough, the only place an old lady is noticeable is in a camera store, particularly if she asks for a special kind of camera to do a special kind of thing, money no

object. There were three large camera stores in town, and
Flavia turned out to have got her camera in the third, naturally. The young man at the counter remembered her perfectly: Northern, perky, knew exactly what she wanted. He
tried to fob her off with an Instamatic, but she wanted a
camera with a telephoto lens and great clarity of focus.
That wasn't the way she put it of course; she said she
wanted to take pictures from a distance and have them
come out well. The man sold her an expensive camera
with a telephoto lens and fully expected to have it back on
his hands the following day, but he never saw her again.
Asked to describe her, he said that she looked like any
other old lady, neat, grandmotherly but firm. She paid with
cash, which surprised him, but she explained that she was
too old to learn to use credit cards." Kate smiled at this,
since she had often seen Flavia use credit cards in restaurants and comment on their usefulness: so much easier to
figure out the tip. Flavia had been covering her tracks.

Finding Flavia herself was a little harder, but not much.
She had stolen one of Georgiana's credit cards and one of
her suitcases, and simply checked into the town's largest
hotel as Georgiana. Naturally, the police didn't think of
that. They had checked hotel registrations, looking for
Flavia's name, or at least an obviously phony name. They
had interviewed the help in all the hotels, but there were
far too many old ladies to make further investigation practical. None of them, in any case, were reported as looking
the least bit "lost." When Kate finally tracked her down,
Flavia was relieved, but also frightened. "I fear for my life,"
she said, "which is rather silly since I had been thinking of
flinging it away. That Divine Church has lost millions of
dollars because of me, and they may decide not to leave
vengeance to the Lord." Kate agreed with her.

When we were all discussing it later in Kate's apartment, armed with fortified refreshment, Great Aunt Flavia was full of praise for Kate for finding her and especially for realizing that she had been responsible for the photograph. "You recognized your advice about invisibility, didn't you, dear?" she said. "How right you were. I loitered around that motel for days, and no one even saw me. People are afraid to speak to old ladies for fear they won't stop talking, and they aren't afraid we're going to be burglars or gunmen. It worked like a charm."

"That's all very well," Kate said, keeping a firm grip on Flavia's exuberance, "but how did you know he would show up, with or without a prostitute?"

"I saw him with her on the street, and I followed him. They were in a car, but I recognized him when they stopped for a light. They turned into the motel a few yards further on. I suppose he thought he was safely distant from his usual stamping ground. They didn't even glance at me when they went into the motel, intent upon what seemed a familiar routine. So I waited until they came out, just to see where they would go. I had called a taxi, and when it came I waited in it, with the meter going, until the Divine Church and his companion emerged. Then I said: 'Follow that car.' I think if I'm ever asked, I'll say that was the high point of my life. After that I bought the camera." Flavia took a long sip of her Scotch and soda.

"How could you be sure the woman was a prostitute?" Kate asked.

"He dropped her off, so I saw where she lived. I asked a man working in her building if he knew her name, because I thought she might be the daughter of a dear friend but I hadn't really seen her very clearly. The man said he thought I must be mistaken, since she wasn't the sort of woman a lady like myself would know. 'Do you mean she's a fallen woman?' I asked him in my most elegant way."

"Flavia, you didn't!"

"I did, and very convincingly too. He told me you might put it that way. So I went off and bought a camera. Fortunately, I didn't have to wait long to get my picture; he was clearly in town for several days. But after I got the picture back and sent it to the newspaper, I thought I'd better hide out. I didn't want to bring any danger on poor Georgiana. I just went right on being invisible in that hotel until you found me. I'm glad you did, Kate; I was getting very tired of that life."

"What set you off on this adventure," I asked, "apart from the thrills of being invisible?" I glared at Kate.

"Hypocrisy and greed, dear. I can't bear people ranting on about sin and old-time values and being born again, when they're just trying to make money like any inside trader on Wall Street. And then, to take money from those poor, old ladies, and pretend you are writing personal letters, when it's all done with computers. Taking advantage of loneliness: I was shocked, really shocked. I thought if the old ladies all over the country knew what sort of man he was, they might think again before sending him money. Really I was just lucky that he picked that place to sin in. Or do you think the Lord was getting tired of him?"

"Well, you certainly started a huge scandal. It may be in the news for weeks."

"I hope it will all have died down by next spring when it's time for my visit to Georgiana," Great Aunt Flavia said.

MURDER WITHOUT A TEXT

At the time of her arraign-
ment, Professor Beatrice Sterling had never set foot in a
criminal court. As a juror—a duty she performed regularly
at the close of whatever academic year she was called—she
had always asked to serve in the civil division. She felt too
far removed from the world of criminals, and, because of
her age (and this was true even when she was younger,
referring as it did more to the times in which she had been
born than to the years she had lived), too distanced from
the ambience of the criminal to judge him (it was almost
always a him) fairly. She was, in short, a woman of tender
conscience and unsullied reputation.

All that was before she was arrested for murder.

Like most middle-class dwellers in Manhattan, therefore,
she had never been through the system, never been treated
like the felon that the DA's office was claiming her to be. It
is a sad truth that those engaged in activity they know to be
criminal—shoddy business practices, drug dealing, protection rackets, contract killings—have quicker access to the

better criminal lawyers. Those unlikely to be accused of anything more serious than jaywalking often know only the lawyer who made their will or, at best, some unpleasant member of a legal firm as distant from the defense of felons as from the legal intricacies of medieval England.

Beatrice Sterling's lawyer was a partner in a corporate law firm; long married to a woman who had gone to school with Beatrice, he had some time ago agreed to make her will as a favor to his wife. His usual practice dealt with the mergers or takeovers of large companies; he had never even proffered legal advice to someone getting a divorce, let alone accused of murder. There was not even a member of his firm knowledgeable about how the criminal system worked at the lower end of Manhattan, next door though it might have been to where their elegant law firm had its being.

The trouble was, until her arraignment, neither Beatrice nor her sister considered any other lawyer. It is always possible that with the best legal advice in the world Beatrice would still have been remanded, but as it happened, she never had any chance of escaping rides to and from Riker's Island in a bus reinforced with mesh wiring, and incarceration in a cell with other women, mostly drug dealers and prostitutes. By that time Beatrice was alternately numb or seized with such rage against the young woman she was supposed to have murdered that her guilt seemed, even to her unhappy corporate counsel, likely.

Professor Beatrice Sterling was accused of having murdered a college senior, a student in a class Beatrice had been teaching at the time the young woman was found bludgeoned to death in her dormitory room. The young woman had hated Beatrice; Beatrice had hated the young woman and, in fact, every young woman in that particular class. She would gladly, as she had unfortunately mentioned to a few dozen people, have watched every one of her students whipped out of town and tarred and feathered as well. She had, however, insisted that she had not committed murder or even laid a finger on the dead girl. This counted for little against the evidence of the others in the class, who claimed, repeatedly and with conviction, that Beatrice had hated them all and was clearly not only vicious but capable of murder.

The police had carried out a careful investigation, putting their most reliable and experienced homicide detectives on the case. These, a man and a woman, decided that they had a better than even case against the lady professor, and, since the case might become high-profile, got an arrest warrant and went to her apartment to arrest her and bring her into the precinct.

It is possible, even at this stage, to avoid being sent to jail, but not if the charge is murder in the second degree (first degree murder is reserved for those who kill policepersons). Those accused of minor misdemeanors are issued a Desk Appearance Ticket and ordered to appear in court some three or four weeks hence. (Sometimes they do, sometimes they don't, but such a choice was not offered to Beatrice, who would certainly have appeared anytime she was ordered to.) She was allowed one phone call, which she made to her sister to ask for a lawyer–a wasted call since the sister, whose name was Cynthia Sterling, had already called the corporate lawyer husband of Beatrice's school friend.

Beatrice was told by the woman detective that it could be anywhere from twenty-four to seventy-two hours until her arraignment and that probably no lawyer could get to her until a half hour before that occurred. Men who go through the system are held during this period in pens behind the courtrooms. Since there are, in the Manhattan criminal system, no pens for women, Beatrice was held in a cell in the precinct. The system happened at that time to be more than usually backed up—and it was usually backed up—so she was not taken directly to Central Booking at One Police Plaza, police headquarters for all the boroughs and Central Booking for Manhattan, until two days had passed.

Neither Beatrice nor her sister Cynthia had ever married, and a more unlikely pair to become caught in the criminal system could not easily be imagined. As Beatrice in jail alternated between numbness and rage, weeping and cold anger, Cynthia came slowly, far too slowly as she later accused herself, to the conclusion that what she needed was help from someone who understood the criminal system.

Beatrice's school friend's husband was useless: less than useless, because he did not know how little he knew. A knowledgeable lawyer could not now save Beatrice from her present incarceration and all the shame and humiliation connected with it, but he or she might be able to offer some worthwhile, perhaps even practical, advice.

We all know more people than we at first realize. Cynthia could have sworn that she knew no one connected with law enforcement or criminal defense even four times removed. She forced herself to sit quietly, and upright, in a chair, calming herself in the manner she had read of as recommended for those undertaking meditation in order to lower their blood pressure. She sat with her feet flat on the floor, her back straight to allow a direct line from the top of her head to the base of her spine, and in this position she repeated, as she thought she remembered from her reading, a single word. Any one-syllable word, if simple relaxation as opposed to religious experience were the aim, would suffice. She chose, not without some sense of irony, the word "law." Faith in law was what, above all, she needed. Slowly repeating this word with her eyes closed and her breathing regular, she bethought herself, as though the word had floated to her from outer space, of Angela Epstein.

Cynthia, after continuing her slow breathing and word repetition for a few seconds out of gratitude, contemplated the wonders of Angela Epstein. She had come to Cynthia's office only a week or two ago to say hello.

Could fate, were there any such thing, have whispered in her ear? Cynthia was the dean in charge of finances at a large, urban college quite different from the elite suburban institution in which Beatrice taught. In that capacity, Cynthia had, in the past, been able to put Angela Epstein in the way of fellowship aid, and Angela, unlike the greater number of her kind, had continued to be grateful. Finding herself in the area of her old college, she had stopped in to greet Cynthia, to thank her for her past help, and to tell Cynthia about her present life. What Angela did—it was something in the investment line—Cynthia could not precisely remember, but some words of Angela's echoed, like the voice of a guardian angel in a legend, in Cynthia's postmeditation ears: "I'm living with a wonderful guy; he's a public defender, and he loves what he does. It's great to live with someone who loves what he does, and who does good things for people caught up in New York's criminal system. Between us, we can afford a loft in Manhattan."

From Information, Cynthia got the number of Angela Epstein. Here, as it was night, she got a message machine. She left as passionate a request for Angela to call back as she could muster; indeed, passion quivered in every syllable. But if Angela and her lover had retired at midnight, they might not return her call until morning, perhaps not until they returned from work the next day.

Cynthia decided—rather, she was seized by a determination—to go and visit Angela herself at that very moment. Perhaps she would not get in; perhaps she would be mugged in the attempt. But with Beatrice behind bars, any action seemed better than no action. She pictured herself banging on the door of their loft until allowed entrance and the chance to plead. She dressed hurriedly, descended to the street, commandeered a taxi, and told the driver to take her to the Lower East Side, insisting over his protests that that was indeed where she wanted to go.

"This time of night, you gotta be outta your mind."

It occurred to Cynthia, even in the midst of her distracted determination, that she had not been driven by an old-fashioned cabdriver for a very long time indeed. He was American, old, shaggy, and wonderfully soothing.

"I have to go now," she said. "Please. Take me."

"It's your funeral, literally. I'm telling you. I wouldn't be out on the streets myself this time of night, except it's my nephew's cab; my nephew's having a baby in the hospital with his wife. It takes two to have a baby these days, I mean to have it, not to start it, if you see what I mean. Me, I drive only by day."

"I see," Cynthia said, blessing him for beginning to drive.

"He's working his way through law school, drives a cab at night. These days, in this city, you don't need to be a lawyer, you need to hire one, and a doctor too while you're at it, I tell him. So he's crazy, so you're crazy. You're not buying drugs, I hope?"

Cynthia assured him that she was not. Was meditation like prayer? Was it answered like prayer? First the name had come to her, then this wonderful cabdriver. Could another miracle happen, that they would hear her pounding on the door and let her in and listen to her story?

Another miracle happened, though not quite that way. As she emerged from the taxi, a couple approached her. They looked at her oddly; she was not, it was to be assumed, a usual type to be seen in this neighborhood at this hour. The couple had also emerged from a taxi, even now departing.

"Dean Sterling!" someone shouted. It was Angela Epstein. "What on earth are you doing here?"

"I'm looking for you," Cynthia said, suddenly unbelievably tired, worn out by all the sudden good fortune that had come her way.

"So ya gonna pay me, or ya forgot and left your purse at home?"

Cynthia came to her senses, apologizing to the cabdriver and the astonished young couple. She reached into her purse and gave the cabdriver a large bill. "For you and your nephew and the baby," she said. "You are wonderful."

"You too," he shouted, taking off with a screech of tires. Cynthia had meant to beg him to return, but she merely shrugged. It was Angela Epstein's young man upon whom she now turned her full attention.

"You are a public defender? You understand the criminal system?" She asked as though he might deny it and turn out to be something wholly useless.

"Yes," he said, taking her arm. "Are you in trouble? Why don't we go upstairs and talk about it?" Over her head, for he was a tall young man, he gave Angela a quizzical look; she made soothing gestures and rushed ahead to open the building door, peering about to see that there were no dangerous types lurking.

"I'm afraid I don't even know your name," Cynthia said.

"My name's Leo," he said. "Leo Fansler. What's yours?"

"Cynthia Sterling. My sister Beatrice Sterling is in jail, accused of murder. And I'm afraid they won't even let her out on bail; that seemed to be the only coherent statement I could get out of the lawyer I called. Will you help us?"

"I'll try," Leo Fansler said.

They got her settled on the couch with a cup of tea and a blanket over her legs because the loft was chilly. Besides, they wanted to do all the easy things they could think of to help her. She had always appeared to Angela as a woman of such power and efficiency, but she now looked the very picture of distraction and disarray, rather—Leo later said to Angela—like the White Queen. (Leo had to explain who the White Queen was. "You've read everything," Angela lovingly accused him. "Not really," he answered. "I just lived for a time with a literary aunt.")

At last Cynthia managed to tell Leo, in answer to his questions, with what her sister was charged, when she had been arrested, whether or not the detectives had had a warrant, and whether she had yet been arraigned. He tried, as gently as possible, to keep her from telling him the whole story from the very beginning. "Not yet," he said. "I'll find out from your sister; I'll talk to her. I'll get the whole story, believe me. But right now all I want to know is where she is, and what's already happened in court."

Cynthia made a noble attempt to be as coherent as possible. To her infinite relief, Leo understood her, interpreted her vague answers, knew what to do.

"Do you know when the arraignment is?" he asked. "Did they tell you, or her?"

"Probably tomorrow, but they can't be sure."

"Okay. I'll be there," Leo said. "Her lawyer will try for bail at the arraignment, but probably won't get it. The chances are she'll be remanded, and we'll try again; we may do better upstairs at the felony arraignment. But if she does get bail for a murder charge, it may be in the neighborhood of a million dollars. Can you raise that much? There are bondsmen. . . ."

"I'll raise it," Cynthia said. "The lawyer already spoke to me about that. The one who doesn't know anything. I think he talked about money because that's all he knows anything about. We'll mortgage our apartment. It's very valuable. It's worth over a million now, though it wasn't when we moved in thirty years ago."

"It takes a while to get a mortgage, even a loan," Leo said, more to himself than her. "I'm going to call you a taxi now; the company will send one if we offer double. Otherwise they avoid this neighborhood at night. You go home and try to get some rest. Meet me in the public defender's office on Centre Street across from the courthouse tomorrow morning at nine. Can you manage that?"

"I could take her," Angela said. "I could be late to work."

"I'll find it," Cynthia said. "Please, you've done enough. I'll meet you there."

"Get off the subway at Chambers Street. Then ask someone the way. Don't take a taxi; you'll be stuck in traffic for hours."

"I'll be there," Cynthia said. "Poor Beatrice. I'll be there. You will let me convince you she's innocent."

"Tomorrow, or maybe even later. The important thing is, you've got someone on your side who knows the system. That's all you have to think about right now. I'm going to try to get you another lawyer for the trial. I know it's impossible, but try not to worry too much."

CYNTHIA ARRIVED AT the public defender's office at nine o'clock. She saw no reason to tell Leo, who came out to the reception desk to meet her, that she had set out at seven and wandered around the confusing streets of lower Manhattan for at least an hour, until a truck driver finally gave her proper directions. Leo led her off to his office, hung up her coat, sat her down, and tried to tell her what had happened so far.

"Where is Beatrice now?" Cynthia asked, before he began.

"Probably on her way in from Central Booking. We haven't much time, so you must listen."

"I am listening," Cynthia said, drawing together all her powers of attention. The time for action had come.

"All right," Leo said. "She was arrested and taken to your precinct, where pedigree information–name, address, and so on–are taken, and a warrant check is made, that is, to see if she is wanted on any other cases. I know, I know, but we're talking about the system here, not your sister. As you'll see when we go to court, most of those arrested have records, and quite a number do not have an address, so she's ahead on that count. The detectives will have questioned your sister extensively, and we can only pray she had the sense not to say anything at all. Any statement she made upon arrest can and will be read out at her arraignment."

"It all seems very unfair," Cynthia said, "taking advantage of people when they're upset."

"That's exactly the point. And even hardened criminals rarely know enough to shut up. I don't know how long she was held in the precinct—I'll find out—but it was as long as they had to wait before Central Booking was ready to process more bodies." Leo ignored the fact that Cynthia had closed her eyes and gone white. He kept on talking to bring her around. "Her prints were then faxed to Albany, where they are matched by computer against all other prints in the state. The result is a rap sheet, which in your sister's case will be encouragingly blank. I assume she has no record." He looked at Cynthia, who nodded certainly. "That's good news for our side when it comes to pleading for bail," Leo said.

"The reason she's now in jail is because the system was backed up; they had to go to the DA's office for a complaint to be drawn up, and because she had to be interviewed by the Criminal Justice Agency." Leo noticed that Cynthia was beginning to look faint. "Hold on," he said. "We're almost finished with this part. She's got a CJA sheet—for Criminal Justice Agency," he added, as faintness was now joined by bewilderment. "Everyone in court, the judge, the DA, your sister's lawyer, will use that sheet. It gives the years at her address, her employment, length of employment, and so on. That's going to help your sister, because she's obviously been a responsible member of the community with a good employment record and a steady address. We're waiting now until all these papers reach the court. We'll try for bail at the arraignment, but don't be hopeful. On a murder charge like this, she'll almost certainly be remanded at arraignment."

"Will you be at the arraignment arguing for her bail?"

"I can't be," Leo said. "She's not eligible for legal aid. But I've got her a lawyer, a woman I went to law school with. She's first-rate, she has worked for the DA, she knows what she's doing, she's smart, and above all, she'll understand where your sister's coming from. She's already gone to the court to be ready to meet with your sister when she's brought in from Central Booking to the arraignment. That's the whole story. Are you okay for now?"

"Will they put her in a cell when she gets here?"

"No. Women aren't put into pens. She'll sit on a bench with other women prisoners at the front of the courtroom. She'll go into a booth there to talk to her lawyer. We're going over there now; you'll see the setup."

"Will she see me?"

"Yes. But you mustn't try to talk to her or to reach her. Sally, that's her lawyer, will tell her about what you've done so far, including finding me. Ready. Here's your coat. Let's go."

"Don't you need a coat?" Leo shook his head. Nothing, he thought, would keep a woman from noticing he didn't wear a coat racing around the courts; no man would ever notice it. It had something to do with female nurturing, Angela would say.

"Do you think you could walk down six flights," he asked, "because the elevators take forever? Good. We're off."

There was a lot happening at the court. Cynthia saw the judge, the DAs, and men in white shirts with guns who Leo said were court officers; they carried the papers between the lawyers and the judge. When Beatrice was brought in front of the judge, holding her hands behind her, Cynthia thought she would weep and never stop. She couldn't hear what any of them said, except for the DA who spoke loud and clear: "The people are serving statement notice. Defendant said: 'I didn't kill her. I loathed her but I didn't kill her. I couldn't kill anyone.' No other notices."

Cynthia looked with agony at Leo.

"Never mind. Not exactly inculpatory. It's always better to shut up, but a protest of innocence is not the worst. Listen now; Sally's asking for bail. The DA asked that she be remanded–sent to jail while awaiting trial. Sally's answering."

"With all due respect, your honor, the ADA's position, while predictable, takes no account of my client's position in the community. The case is not strong against my client; the major evidence is circumstantial. We have every intention of fighting this case. My client not only has no record, but is a long-honored professor in a well-established and well-known institution of higher education. She has been a member of the community and has lived at the same address for many years. There can be no question of my client's returning. We ask that bail be set sufficient to insure that return, but not excessive. My client is a woman in her late fifties who is innocent and intends to prove it." There was more, but Cynthia seemed unable any longer to listen. Leo had said there was little hope for bail at this point. She tried to send thought waves of encouragement and support to Beatrice, but the sight of her back with her hands held together behind her was devastating.

The judge spoke with–Cynthia might have felt under other circumstances–admirable clarity. "The defendant is remanded. Adjourned to AP–17, January sixth, for grand jury action."

That was that. Beatrice was led away, and Cynthia wept.

"It won't be too long," Leo said, trying to find some words of comfort. "The law does not allow anyone to be kept more than one hundred forty-four hours after arrest without an indictment. And now she has a lawyer who knows what she's doing, and who will, with any luck, get bail for her after her felony arraignment upstairs. You go home and try to be ready to raise it. At least a million; that's a guess, but probably a good one. Can you get home all right?" Cynthia looked at where Beatrice had been, but she was gone. She saw the booths–like confessionals, she thought–where Beatrice might have talked to her lawyer before Leo had brought her. But Leo hurried her out; he was already late for another hearing in another court.

Later Leo and Sally met for lunch in a Chinese restaurant on Mulberry Street. Sally was not encouraging. "Am I sure she didn't do it? No, I'm not sure, so what is a jury going to make of her? Talk about reasonable doubt: I'd have less doubt if I saw the cat licking its lips before an empty birdcage. Leo, my love, my treasure, take my advice: start thinking about a plea in this case. She'll get eight and a third to twenty-five if she's maxed out on a manslaughter plea, with parole after eight and a third. Otherwise, we're talking fifteen to life. Think of Jean Harris."

"Jean Harris shot her lover."

"That's more excusable than bludgeoning to death a twenty-year-old girl."

"What happened exactly?"

"According to the DA? The girl was found dead in her dormitory room on a Saturday night. The dormitory was close to empty, and no one saw anything, except some boy on his way out who saw an old lady, and picked Professor B out of a lineup. A hell of a lot of good her corporate lawyer did her there. Professor B says she was home, sister away at some institutional revel. Every one of the girl's friends has testified that Professor B hated her, though only slightly more than she hated the other girls in her seminar. Something to do with women's studies, more's the pity."

"That's all the DA's got?"

"An eyewitness, a lack of other suspects, and Professor

B's prints all over the girl's notebook. Even Daphne's friends admit she went rather far in goading the old lady, but that hardly excuses murder. It's not as though we're dealing with the battered woman syndrome here. That's how it is, Leo. We'll have to plead her out."

"THANKS FOR AGREEING to a Japanese restaurant," Leo said. "I know it's not your thing. I needed some raw fish: brain food. Also you like the martinis here; I think you better have two before I start on my story."

Kate Fansler sipped from the one she had already ordered and contemplated Leo. He had said he wanted advice; the question was, about what? Kate considered the role of aunt far superior to that of parent, which did not alter the fact that the young made her nervous. This advice, however, turned out not to be about the young.

"It doesn't sound like a very strong case against her," Kate said, when Leo had told her the story and consumed several yellowback somethings; he went on to eel.

"It's not, but it's the sort of case they'll win. They'll bring on all the girl's friends, and what's on Beatrice's side? A devoted sister, and all the stereotypes in the world to tell you she had a fit of frantic jealousy and knocked the girl's head in."

"You sound rather involved."

"I'm always involved; that's why I'm so good at what I do, and why it's interesting. I also know how to get uninvolved at five o'clock and go home, unlike high-class lawyers."

"So Sally's arguments have a certain cogency."

"Naturally. That's the trouble. It's a little early to tell, but it looks to me like either she cops or, as my clients say, she'll blow trial and get a life term. As far as I can see it's a dilemma with only one way out. Find the real killer. Right up your alley, I rather thought."

Kate, who had decided on only one martini, waved for the waiter and ordered another. "I've known you so long," she said, "that I'm not going to exchange debating points. We can both take it as said. If I wanted to talk with your murderer, would I have to go out to Riker's Island?"

"No. Anyway, I'm pretty sure Sally will get bail after the indictment, if we have any luck at all with the judge. There's every reason not to keep the old gal in jail, and Sally can be very persuasive. In which case you can visit her in the apartment they have just mortgaged to get the bail."

"Leo, I want one thing perfectly clear. . . ."

"As you said, dear Aunt Kate, we know the debating points. Just talk to the elderly sisters, together, separately, and let me know what you decide. End of discussion, unless, of course, you decide they're innocent and I can help."

"I thought it was just one of them?"

"It is, but Cynthia's the one I met first, so I sort of think of them as a pair. I've never met Beatrice, just caught sight of her with the other women prisoners at the arraignment. But I have met Cynthia, I've heard Angela on Cynthia, and I'm not ready to believe that Cynthia's sister could have murdered anyone."

LEO HAD TOLD Kate that for a woman of Professor Beatrice Sterling's background, experience of the criminal system would be a nightmare; indeed, Beatrice, as she asked Kate to call her, had the look of someone who has seen horrors. They were meeting in the sisters' apartment after bail had been granted. Cynthia, now that Beatrice was home, was clearly taking the tack that a good dose of normality was what was needed, and she was providing it, with a kind of courageous pretense at cooperation from Beatrice that touched Kate, who allowed a certain amount of desultory chatter to go on while she reviewed the facts in her mind.

Burglary had always been a possibility, but it was considered an unlikely one. The victim's wallet had not been taken, though the cash, if any, had. Her college ID, credit cards, and a bank card remained. Pictures that had been in the wallet had been vigorously torn apart and scattered over the body. Her college friends, although they knew the most intimate facts of her life, as was usual these days, did not know how much money she usually carried or if anything else was missing from her wallet. She had been bludgeoned with a tennis award—a metal statue of a young woman swinging a racket—that had been heavily weighted at the base. The assailant had worn gloves. What had doomed Beatrice was not so much these facts, not even the identification by the young man (though this was crushing), but the record of deep dislike between the victim and the accused that no one, not even the accused, denied.

Motive is not enough for a conviction, but, as Leo had put it, the grounds for reasonable doubt were also, given the likely testimony of the victim's friends, slim. Kate put down her teacup and started to speak of what faced them.

"You are our last hope," Cynthia said, before Kate could begin.

"If that is true," Kate answered, looking directly into the eyes of first one and then the other, "then you are going to have to put up with my endless questions, and with retelling your story until you think even jail would be preferable. Now, let's start at the beginning, with a description of this seminar itself. How did you come to teach it? Were these students you had known before? What was the subject? I want every detail you can think of, and then some. Start at the beginning."

Beatrice took a deep breath, and kept her eyes on her hands, folded in her lap. "I didn't know these particular students at all," she said, "and I didn't particularly want to teach that seminar. For two reasons," she added, catching Kate's "Why?" before it was spoken. "It was in women's studies, which I have never taught. I'm a feminist, but my field is early Christian history, and I have not much expertise about contemporary feminist scholarship. The seminar was for writing honors theses in women's studies, which meant there were no texts; in addition, the students were all doing subjects in sociology or political science or anthropology, and I know little of these fields beyond their relation to my own rather ancient interests. I had worked hard, and under some unpleasant opposition, to help establish women's studies at our college, so I had little excuse not to take my turn in directing this seminar; in any case, there was no one else available. There were twelve students, all seniors, and yes, it did occur to me to relate it to the Last Supper, which I mention only because you will then understand what the seminar evoked in me." A sigh escaped, but Beatrice, with an encouraging pat from Cynthia, continued.

"The young are rude today; anyone who teaches undergraduates can tell you that. They are not so much aggressively rude as inconsiderate, as though no perspective but theirs existed. The odd part of this is that the most radical students, those who talk of little but the poor and the racially oppressed, are, if anything, ruder than the others, courtesy being beneath them. Forgive me if I rant a bit, but you wanted to hear all this.

"The point is, they hated me on sight and I them. Well, that's an exaggeration. But when I tried to suggest what seemed to me minimal scholarly standards, they sneered. Quite literally, they sneered. I talked this over with the head of women's studies, and she admitted that they are known to be an unruly bunch, and that they had not wanted me for their seminar, but she couldn't do anything except cheer me on. They spoke about early feminists, like me, as though we were a bunch of co-opted creeps. Worst of all, they never talked to me or asked me anything; they addressed each other, turning their backs on me. You're a teacher, so perhaps this will sound less silly to you than to the police. It was the kind of rudeness that is close to rape. Or murder. Oh, don't think I don't usually run quite successful classes; I do. Students like me. Of course, my students are self-selected: they're interested in the subject, which they elect to take. But even when I teach a required history survey, I do well. I'm not as intimate with the students as some of the younger teachers, and I regret that, but I grew up in a different time, and it seems best to be oneself and not pretend to feelings one doesn't have. Do you agree?"

Kate nodded her agreement.

"The dead girl—they called each other only by their first names, and hers was Daphne, but I remembered *her* last name (which the police found suspicious) because it was Potter-Jones, and that sounded to me like something out of a drama from the BBC—she was the rudest of the lot and was writing on prostitutes, or, as they insisted on calling them, sex workers. I should add that all their subjects were

enormous, totally unsuitable for undergraduates, and
entirely composed of oral history. All history, all previously published research, was lies. They would talk to real
sex workers, real homeless women, real victims of botched
abortions, that sort of thing. When I suggested some academic research, they positively snorted. Daphne said that
being a sex worker was exactly like being a secretary–they
were equally humiliating jobs–but at least we might try to
see that sex workers got fringe benefits. My only private
conversation, if you can call it that–they never, any of
them, came to my office hours or consulted me for a
minute–was with Daphne. She had been advised at a seminar to pretend to be a sex worker and try to get into a
'house' so that she might meet some prostitutes; she had,
not surprisingly to me but apparently to her and all the
others, found it difficult to get prostitutes to talk to her. I
took her aside at the end of the class and told her I thought
that might be rather dangerous. She laughed, and said she
had told her mother, who thought it was a great idea. I
know all this may sound exaggerated or even the wander-
ings of a demented person, but this is, I promise you, a
straightforward rendition of my experience. I have spared
you some details, considering them repetitive. No doubt
you get the picture. It occurred to me, when I was in Riker's
Island, that perhaps I might now be of some interest to the
members of the seminar, except of course that they thought
I had murdered their friend, so I failed to interest them
even as an accused murderer. Cynthia thought I oughtn't to
mention that, but my view is if, knowing it all, you can't
believe me, I might as well plead to manslaughter as my
young but clearly smart lawyer urges."

Kate did not break for some minutes the silence that fell
upon them. She was trying to order her perceptions, to

analyze her responses. Could the hate Beatrice felt have driven her to violence? Kate put that thought temporarily on hold. "Tell me about the night of the murder," she said. "You were here the whole time alone. Is that the whole truth?"

"All of it. The irony is, Cynthia tried to persuade me to go with her to the party, which she thought might be better than most. I almost went, but I had papers to correct, and in the end I stayed home, thereby sacrificing my perfect alibi. Do you think the moral is: Always accept invitations?"

"When did you last see Daphne?"

"I last saw them all the day before, at the meeting of the seminar. I think they had been told that I would give them a grade, and that attendance would count. The director was probably trying to help me, but that of course only increased their resentment, which increased mine. I don't want to exaggerate, but at the same time you should know that this was the worst teaching experience I have ever had."

"Were you shocked when that young man picked you out of the lineup?"

"At the time, yes, shocked and horrified. But soon after it all began to seem like a Kafka novel; I wasn't guilty, but that didn't matter. They would arrange it all so that I was condemned. And they had found my fingerprints on Daphne's notebook; it was like mine, and I had picked it up by mistake at the last seminar. Daphne always sat next to me, I never knew why, but I supposed because from there, as I was at the head of the table, she could most readily turn her back to me and address her comrades. I had opened her notebook before I saw my mistake; I've no doubt I left my fingerprints all over it. But that also told against me. You might as well hear the worst. Before I was arrested, I would have told you that I was incapable of bludgeoning anyone to death. Now, I think I am quite capable of it."

SOME DAYS LATER Kate summoned Leo to dinner, requesting that he bring along Beatrice's lawyer; they met this time in an Italian restaurant: Kate's tolerance for watching Leo consume raw fish had its limits. Sally had clearly come prepared for Kate's admission that any defense would be quixotic, if not fatal.

"I'm not so sure," Kate told her. "There's nothing easy about this case. Beatrice's reaction to this seminar was unquestionably excessive; on the other hand, had murder not occurred, she would probably have forgotten the whole thing by now. No doubt her words would seem extreme to anyone who had not labored long in the academic vineyards. I'll only mention that when Beatrice took up teaching, she saw respect for the scholar as one of the perks of the job; she has, in addition, risked much and undergone considerable pain as an early feminist. To her, it seems as though all this has become less than nothing. Add that to what may well be a period of personal depression, and you have this reaction. Do we also have murder? I don't think so, and for three reasons.

"First, I think the last thing Beatrice would do would be to go to that girl's room under any pretense whatsoever; Beatrice claims never to have entered a dormitory and I believe her. I know, so far nothing counts that much with you"–Kate held up a cautioning hand to Sally–"but I have two other reasons, both of them, I think, persuasive. One, I purchased a cheap gray wig, donned some rather raggy clothes, and wandered into the dorm where Beatrice was supposedly spotted. I'm prepared to stand in a line and see if that young man or anyone else picks me out: to youth one gray-haired, frumpish woman looks very like another. Doffing my wig, donning my usual dress, I returned to the dormitory half an hour later; needless to say, no one recognized me. I was there this time to interview Daphne's roommate, who was also in the seminar. She told me how close she and Daphne were—they even looked alike—and how devastated she was. She, it turned out, was writing on the homeless and had had almost as much difficulty in interviewing her objects of oral history as had Daphne. Her animus against Beatrice was pronounced, but that was hardly surprising. I asked how her paper was going; she had gotten an extension under the circumstances, but had, in fact, found only one homeless woman to interview. She told me about her. No, don't interrupt. Good pasta, isn't it?

"I tried to find this homeless woman and failed, but I did get a description. I would suggest that when you find her, she and some others similarly dressed be put in the lineup with Beatrice to let that young man reconsider. No, that isn't my clincher. Here's my clincher." Kate took a sip of wine and sat back for a moment.

"I noticed that Daphne had a MasterCard, an American Express card, and no VISA card. Now that's perfectly possible—not all of us carry every card—but I was, as you know, grasping at straws, or at least thinnish reeds. Nudged by me, the police arranged to see every credit card bill that came in after Daphne's death. That merely seemed like another crazy idea of the lady detective, until yesterday. The VISA bill came in yesterday. Here it is." Kate passed it to Sally; Leo looked at it too. "See anything of interest?" Kate asked.

"Yes," Sally said. "There's a charge during the days when Beatrice was in Riker's Island; two, in fact. But are these charges always recorded on the day they're charged?"

"Those from supermarkets are," Kate said. "I've checked

with this particular supermarket, which is in a shopping center near the college. Beatrice never goes there, since she lives in the city, but it's also doubtful that Daphne did; she was, in any case, dead at the time of this charge."

"Let me be sure I have this right," Leo said, as Sally continued to stare at the bill. "You're saying Daphne's roommate's homeless interviewee killed Daphne, tore up the pictures in anger, perhaps mistook Daphne for her roommate or was too full of rage to care, stole the cash and one credit card that she later used to buy food at a supermarket. The police will have to find her. That's for sure."

"I think if the police put their minds to it, they'll find more evidence still. What *you've* got to do, Sally, after you've got the charges against Beatrice dismissed, is take up the defense of the homeless woman. I'll pay the legal costs. Given one of those uppity girls questioning and patronizing her, and probably inviting her once or twice to their comfy dormitory room, I should think you'd get her a suspended sentence at the very least. Extreme provocation."

"Please God she hasn't got previous convictions," Sally said.

"I doubt it," Kate said. "It could well take an undergraduate to send even the most benign homeless person over the edge. The trouble with the police," she added sanctimoniously, "is that they've never tried to teach a class without a text. One can do nothing without the proper equipment, as they should be the first to understand. I have urged Beatrice to write a calm letter to the director of women's studies suggesting an entire revamping of the senior thesis seminar. They must require texts. Under the circumstances, it seems the least they can do.

"More wine?"

Who Shot

Mrs. Byron Boyd?

༄

Mark Stampede wrote the most macho books that could still pass for crime fiction, at least as most of the other members of the Crime Writers' Association of America defined it. Mariana Phillips's mystery novels, while far from what anyone could call ladylike or, heaven forfend, romantic, deprecated male violence and brought into fictional disrepute the male vision that classed women, in E. M. Forster's immortal words, with motor cars if they were attractive and with eye flies if they were not. Mark Stampede worked out in a gym, with the result that the muscles in his upper body were highly developed while his protruding belly betrayed his voracious appetite and ready thirst. Mariana Phillips, who possessed neither biceps nor belly, tended to place women at the center of her fictions, pleasant, kindly men at the periphery, and macho men either as villains or, preferably, as corpses. How the two of them turned up on one platform in a very large hall during the course of a rather high-flown fiction writers' series was a question no one would answer, either when asked politely at the beginning of the event by Mariana Phillips, with considerably less gallantry during the course of the event by Stampede, or with no courtesy at all by the police as the evening wore on.

Mariana Phillips, a woman of honor and a scholar of sorts, had read at least two of Stampede's books before the panel to see what she was up against, and out of courtesy. Stampede had never heard of Phillips's books, considered courtesy an effete maneuver to enslave men, and would not have read a syllable Phillips wrote if no other words had been available on the proverbial desert island.

The event or panel never did end, leaving forever unresolved the question of how in the world anyone was going to get out of this unfortunate confrontation; rather it was interrupted, after the two panelists had disagreed with one another on every possible subject in an atmosphere growing increasingly unpleasant, by a gunshot. For whom the bullet was intended was unclear: indeed, establishing that was the first priority of the police and the unfortunate institution sponsoring the event. What was unhappily obvious was who the bullet hit: an elderly woman who had been persuaded at the last moment to moderate the panel. Perhaps, given the youth-worshipping qualities of our culture, "middle-aged" was the kinder phrase for the victim, although, as Mark Stampede had earlier made clear in tones that reverberated throughout the acoustically alive hall, dames over thirty-five were like Australia: everyone knew it was down there and nobody gave a damn.

The original moderator had been held up by a personal crisis, and the dead woman, Mrs. Byron Boyd (as she preferred to be called) had been persuaded to preside in his place at the latest possible moment. She was on the "hostess" committee, and near to hand when the telephone message announcing his inability to arrive was received from the original moderator.

The police assumed that the gunperson, as the officer in charge said with a sneer, was mad, personally connected to the victim, or possibly both. Everyone else in the hall assumed that an alter ego of Mark Stampede's had supposed himself (or herself) to be aiming at Mariana Phillips and had shot another female non–sex object by mistake. If women are all the same in the dark, older women are all the same in the light. That seemed the readiest explanation, if explanation it could be called. No one was prepared to believe that someone in the audience had shot Mrs. Boyd out of frustration with the evening's event. Audiences have been known to snarl at and desert speakers; they do not usually shoot them, having easier means of revenge at hand, such as refusing to buy or even read the speakers' books and advising everyone they know to the same course.

The police, while permitting no one in the audience to leave until names and addresses could be recorded and probable witnesses identified, searched the premises and found the murder weapon in a wastebasket in the women's room. Since that room had, it eventually transpired, been deserted at the time of the shot and immediately afterward, this did not necessarily point to a woman murderer. The gun itself was the sort that can be illegally purchased in all states, and legally purchased in most. It had been wiped clean, although the chance of a gun bearing identifiable prints is, detective fiction to the contrary, small. The police settled down to the long process of listing all those present.

Mark Stampede, clearly identified and innocent, since in the sight of all those people he certainly did not wield a gun, nor could he have shot anyone else on the platform from the position he himself occupied, was allowed to depart. Mariana Phillips, who might have chosen to leave on the same grounds, remained out of sympathy with the dead woman and because she had an abiding interest in other people, their actions and reactions. So she stood for a good while just looking on, and finally subsided into a chair some member of the audience, now standing and swirling about, had deserted.

"THE GENERAL IDEA," Kate Fansler said some days later, having been called in for consultation by her friend Mariana Phillips, "seems to be that whoever shot the gun was aiming at you."

"But why? I may not be universally loved, but I'm hardly hated enough to justify murder." Mariana smiled, indicating that the thought of being worth murdering was not wholly unpleasing. "Thank you for coming to talk about it. It's remarkably hard to think about anything else. Maybe you can help me to talk it out. Maybe," she added, "you can even figure it out. In my opinion, the whole thing was a miserable fluke, an unpremeditated, unmotivated, therefore undetectable crime."

"The general impression I get from the newspapers," Kate said, "is that admirers of Stampede—or the creature himself—are so distressed at his losing sales to 'the mob of scribbling women,' as Hawthorne called them, that they are gunning down the competition: the manly solution to all such problems."

"Stampede is the one person who couldn't have shot her, except for me," Mariana said. "The angle was all wrong; anyway, we would have been seen by five hundred people."

"A hit man," Kate said, with a certain satisfaction. "I haven't come across one before, not in what is so charmingly called real life. I thought they operated only in spy novels and Mafia warfare. Was the poor woman's family there?"

"No. I think the police were trying to get on to her husband. Her children are grown and scattered."

"Did you know her at all well?"

"Not really," Mariana said. "You know how it is. She arranges the reception that always follows these events: wine, cheese, cookies. She's the one who sees that the books of the speakers are available for purchase and autographing. She stands about being gracious. Very old-fashioned; this is her form of good works. I don't even know her first name; I just always said 'Hello, Mrs. Boyd' and passed right along. Wait a minute, I do know her first name: it's Marilee. She did mention that our names were alike. Do you suppose she was a secret admirer of Mark Stampede? She certainly can't have taken to me; I've never had a character in any book who called herself by her husband's name; I'm not her sort at all, really."

"People have an infinite capacity to enjoy books while ignoring the message they find provocative. Someone once said of Shaw's plays that they were revolutionary messages covered with chocolate, but that the audiences licked off the chocolate and left the message. They always wanted Eliza to marry Higgins despite all Shaw's efforts, and still do: Remember *My Fair Lady*?"

"Where do you pick up all this miscellaneous information?"

"I've been a magpie from birth. Here's another example. I just read that Anna Freud, who liked detective novels, only admired books with male heroes, in fact, only fantasized herself as a male hero. But later in life she was willing to read even detective novels with a female detective. See what I mean? Now tell me more about last night."

"Well, after a while I went back up to the stage and looked down from there. The body had been removed, and the police had finished protecting the area. Whoever the murderer was, he or she had certainly not been on the platform when the shot was fired."

"Did you see anyone else on the platform when you went back there?"

"Yes. A young man named Elmer Roth. I never imagined anyone was named Elmer anymore, and I used to watch him as though he'd come from another planet. He had stood about with us—that is, with me and Stampede—while they hurriedly recruited Mrs. Byron Boyd, and he'd tried, with little success, to make conversation. Well, hardly conversation: chitchat. 'We are an ill-suited pair,' I said to Stampede, trying to be minimally friendly. 'I didn't know who else would be on the program when I agreed to appear. Did you?' Stampede answered that question succinctly with a howl of dismay. It occurred to me that Stampede was literally frightened of post-nubile women: either he was with the boys or he was anticipating a good lay. Any other situation was filled with terror."

"Is Mark Stampede married?"

"Not that I know of. Anyway, afterward, Elmer Roth said to me sort of plaintively, 'I thought it would be a real discussion.' I had the feeling he had decided to explain it to me in anticipation of explaining it to the world. 'I thought you both might read a bit from your works and then discuss the function of gender roles in crime fiction. It doesn't,' he added ruefully, but then everything he said was rueful, 'seem to have been one of the century's great ideas.' "

"It was a good enough idea," Kate said. "He just picked rather extreme examples of the possible points of view. My own feeling, though I'm a friend of yours and therefore hardly unbiased, is that you were prepared to be courteous at least, but Stampede responded like a man in a brothel who's been forced to perform with the owner's grandmother. Outraged, I mean. Not getting his rightful desserts. That, at least, was what I gathered from the account in *The Village Voice*. He apparently told someone he was tired of being 'pussy-whipped.' Quite a pungent phrase, that."

"Anyway," Mariana went on, "Elmer was clearly worried that everyone would remember that it was his idea, and blame the whole thing on him. I didn't even realize it was his idea, so I told him not to worry."

"After all," Kate said, "there have been unpleasantnesses on other platforms before this, but no one was shot."

"Poor Elmer said he kept thinking the whole thing was a joke, and that Mrs. Boyd would get up and walk away. I knew exactly what he meant. Do you think someone could have planned a joke, and a real bullet got into the gun by mistake?"

"I'm not sure that's possible, but it's an interesting suggestion," Kate said. "I'll ask Reed."

"Elmer said he felt awfully guilty, because I'd agreed to be on this panel as a favor to him, and I might very well be dead."

"Poor baby," Kate said. "I feel sorry for him. I have to admit it's a bit harder to summon up some real compassion for Mrs. Byron Boyd." This was due, Kate realized, to a certain unreality about the lady or, if it came to that, a certain impression that the whole episode was some trick with mirrors that would ultimately be revealed in all its contrivance. It still seemed imaginable that Mrs. Byron Boyd had sat up in the mortuary van and said, "Well, that joke worked rather well."

Not that the accounts in the papers allowed any such fantasy. Mrs. Byron Boyd's obituaries were lengthy, as were the articles about the shooting. Mrs. Boyd, the newspapers reported, had been shot through the chest and had died within moments. She had, quite literally, never known what hit her. Unlike soldiers and gangwarfarers, she had never braced herself for attack. People in her world were never shot.

"REED," KATE ASKED him that evening, after she had told him about her talk with Mariana Phillips, "is it possible that someone could have been shooting a blank to create drama or for whatever reason, and killed her by mistake because someone else had put a bullet in the gun?"

"It's possible, the way it's possible you'll win the New York State lottery," Reed said. "Apart from all the technical problems, and they are many, the chances of the bullet hitting her in the chest, apparently in the heart or lungs, when shot by someone not really aiming and perhaps not able to aim that precisely—I've lost the end of the sentence; I'll leave you to finish it."

"That's what I thought you would say," Kate sighed.

"How much does Mariana know about Mark Stampede?" Reed asked.

"I asked her that," Kate said. "She doesn't know much of anything—nothing that everyone who reads mysteries and hears talk of crime novels doesn't know. He's supposed to be a pretty rough character, and certainly his remarks that night bear that out. But maybe it's all a public image, and at home he's an angel boy with a cozy wife and five adoring children, all kept strictly out of the limelight. I did ask her if she knew anyone who knows him. She finally came up with someone she knew on a Crime Writers' Association committee who had actually mentioned that Stampede also served on it."

"And you got his name and plan to go to see him."

"Of course," Kate said. "Not that anything will come of it. But I do have to find out more about Stampede. I don't even suppose that can be his real name. As it happens, Larry Donahue has agreed to see me tomorrow. He's a mildly unsuccessful writer, happy to exchange what information he has for a few drinks, like all of his happy breed. And after all, writers can't just stand around and watch each other be shot."

"Good luck," Reed said.

"STAMPEDE IS HIS REAL NAME," Larry Donahue said as he was served with his second martini. Kate could not decide if he had never heard that hard drinking had gone out, or if he had reverted. He was a young man in his thirties, and Kate had long since noticed that members of his generation often lived as though the decades between the Fifties and the Eighties had never been, to say nothing of earlier history. "Somebody asked him at the committee meeting. I think it may have inspired him in some sort of way. He's not a bad guy, really, if you're willing to judge men by their camaraderie with other men, and not their professed opinions of women. His were simplistic: young women were rated one to ten; older women were not a fit subject of conversation or contemplation. But you had the feeling this was all an act he had tried on for size and fit into perfectly. Who knows how many he might have tried on before?"

"How old is he?" Kate asked.

"Middle to late fifties, I would say."

"It wasn't easy to find a picture of him," Kate said.

"There's a picture on the jackets of his recent books, if you can locate a hardcover copy. He's developed a real style. Gold chain, open-necked shirt with sleeves rolled up. I think he dyes his hair. He's definitely on the muscly side, though heavy. Was that what you wanted to know?"

"If I knew what I wanted to know, I'd be better off. You weren't there that night?"

"No; I don't go to those writers' series things much. Mostly I just sit there alternately bored and envious," he said frankly. "I take it the police haven't got anywhere."

"One can hardly blame them," Kate said. "My husband is with the DA, so I have something of an inside track. The obvious suspect, Stampede, couldn't have done it, and the slightly less obvious suspect, Mr. Byron Boyd, turned out to have to be attending a Republican fund-raising dinner in the presence of at least two hundred people." Kate did not bother to add that her favorite suspect, the scheduled moderator who had canceled at the last minute, had spent the operative time at the bedside of his son, who had been in an automobile accident. "We seem to have the perfect crime," she said, "which leads to the uncomfortable conclusion that some lunatic decided to see if he or she could shoot someone in public and get away with it, did shoot and did get away with it. Are Stampede's books very successful?"

"Madly so," Larry Donahue said, looking at his empty glass.

"Would you like another?" Kate asked. Whether Larry Donahue would be more informative drunk or sober was a neat question. Apparently Donahue, considering it, decided to compromise.

"I'll have a beer," he said. "Money was what it was all

about, Stampede always said. Anyone who said any different was either a liar or a fool, and doubly so if a writer of crime fiction. His novels sold to the movies and television, and he loved to sneer at the whole crazy process of film-making, but he always said you didn't make much money from movies and TV. I never knew whether to believe him or not."

"Is he married?"

"Legally, I think, but he's frank to say he just stays married to protect himself from having to marry someone else. If his wife doesn't mind, why should anyone else? is my thought." To Kate's relief he sipped at his beer slowly.

"What is he like at meetings, for example?" she asked.

"There have only been one or two, about nominating people for the board of the Crime Writers' Association. Stampede got on to see we didn't get too many women. His ideas were not well received, so I guess he probably won't come anymore. He liked to say that the best rules of detection were laid down by a priest, and that only Roman Catholics truly understood deception. It's hard to tell whether he's serious or just trying to make a point in a tongue-in-cheek sort of way."

"Do you think he's crazy?"

"Not a chance. He's one of those people like stand-up comics who insult everyone and say things no one is supposed to say; he wants to make an impression and he certainly does." And Kate got nothing more of interest out of him.

KATE HAD MET Mariana Phillips in graduate school, shortly before Mariana abandoned her pursuit of a doctorate in history for the more immediate rewards of popular fiction. Mariana had felt it natural to consult Kate after the crime, and was not amused when Kate pointed out that this was more Mariana's kind of crime than hers. After talking to Larry Donahue, Kate settled down to contemplation of the police reports on witnesses, which Reed had allowed her to see. These were not very helpful, to put it at its most gracious, which was hardly how Kate put it to Reed.

"That, my dear," he responded, "is why they let me waft them before your eyes. All amateur insights welcome, if suitably anonymous. I trust you will have some." Kate stuck out her tongue at him.

"There's nothing here about Stampede himself," she said.

"That probably means he doesn't have a criminal record. I'm sure they ran it through the computer."

"Haven't they put together anything on his life?" Kate asked. "Mariana tells me they've been asking around about her, or so she gathers from her friends' reports. I'd even like to know when and where Stampede was born, and all that sort of thing."

"I'll see what I can do," Reed said. "I'm sorry I referred to amateur insights."

"Don't be. I'm beginning to think that's exactly what's needed here." And she winked. It always worried Reed when Kate winked.

"DO YOU TELL the police or do I?" Kate asked Reed, some days later. It was a rhetorical question; Reed would, of course, tell them, if there was anything to tell. Kate had her own ways of announcing things.

"You've solved it, figured it out, discovered how it was done?" Reed said.

"Certainly," Kate said. "Whether you have enough to arrest him on is another question. That, I am glad to say, is not my problem. I'm a detective, not a lawyer, and as you so truthfully pointed out, an amateur detective at that."

"Who might we be thinking of arresting?" Reed asked, rather against his will.

"Stampede, of course," Kate said. She told Reed all about it, and he, editing her deductions down from their literary heights, told them at the DA's office. They had no trouble with the prosecution; Stampede turned out to have left a trail the rawest of detectives could follow. It was all circumstantial evidence at first, of course, but whatever the police might say, that was the kind of evidence they liked best.

"EXPLAIN IT TO ME CAREFULLY," Mariana Phillips said. "I thought Stampede was the one guy who couldn't possibly have done it. Any more than I could."

"Exactly. So either he didn't do it, or he wasn't standing next to you on the platform."

"As you say, 'exactly.' So?"

"Have you ever heard of Ronald Knox?"

"I think so. Didn't Evelyn Waugh write his biography? I remember Waugh said in the introduction that since the clergy are notoriously longer-lived than the laity, he'd never expected to survive Knox and be his biographer."

"Correct. Knox was a Roman Catholic priest."

"Kate, are we both in the same conversation?"

"In addition to being a priest," Kate continued, ignoring this, "Monsignor Ronald Knox wrote several detective stories, and the 'Ten Commandments of Detection' for all other such authors of detective fiction. Let me read you the tenth." Here Kate paused for emphasis, holding her text in front of her. She read:

"Ten (written as a Roman numeral, naturally): '*Twin brothers, and doubles generally, must not appear unless we have been duly prepared for them.* The dodge is too easy, and the supposition too improbable. I would add as a rider, that no criminal should be credited with exceptional powers of disguise unless we have had fair warning that he or she was accustomed to making up for the stage. How admirably is this indicated, for example, in *Trent's Last Case.*' " Kate stopped and look at Mariana in triumph.

"Had Stampede been accustomed to make up for the stage?"

"No. But he has been involved a great deal lately with moviemaking, both for television and for the larger screen. It was child's play to pick up the tricks and maybe even the actual makeup from around the various sets."

Mariana looked so bewildered that Kate went on without waiting for her to speak.

"Making someone up to look like Stampede was easy, when you come to think of it. He looks like every tough Irishman you've ever seen in a theater, complete with beer belly and gold chain. A travesty, of course, but that's what Stampede was after. Much easier to make two chaps look the same if they're both travesties."

"And which one was really Stampede?"

"The one who shot you, of course. That is, he meant to shoot you, but he probably wasn't following the events on the stage too closely, and when he chose his moment the wrong middle-aged woman was at the podium, intro-ducing a new stage in the proceedings. I think you better dedicate your next book to the memory of Mrs. Byron Boyd; she died in your place. No doubt a man capable of the extreme remarks Stampede liked to bellow forth couldn't tell one dame from another."

"But why did he want to shoot me?"

"You represent the mob of scribbling women. He's one of those men who like to think women are ruining the comfortable world men have made for themselves. They can't believe they haven't a divine right to the center of the stage and the making of all the rules. There are up to ten of them in any academic department in any university. They've all dreamed Stampede's dream, believe me. His was supposed to be the perfect crime, and symbolic into the bargain. He reckoned without me, however, poor man. The hope is that he will never know I had anything to do with finding him out."

"Couldn't the police have done that?"

"Not really; they all think, like Monsignor Knox, that invention cannot attempt what life rarely offers. Stampede had the perfect alibi, and that was that. They undoubtedly would have attributed the shooting to a homicidal maniac, if you hadn't happened to know me."

"No wonder the Stampede on the stage never mentioned any of my books. That would have been too great a demand on the actor's abilities. Insults are easier to deliver convincingly."

"Now you see how it was done."

"How long do you think he had been planning it?"

"Quite a while, I would say. At least it explains why he agreed to so unlikely an event as a panel with the two of you discussing gender roles in detective fiction."

"Poor Elmer Roth."

"Poor Mrs. Byron Boyd," Kate rather perfunctorily said.

"But wasn't Stampede in danger of being blackmailed by the fellow on the stage, impersonating him?"

"I doubt it. The actor probably didn't know why he was there, and even after the shot, he may not have suspected. Even if he did, Stampede had only to tell him to go ahead and publish. Who was to know which of them fired the shot or thought the whole thing up? Nothing to stop Stampede from saying it was the actor's idea in the first place.

After all, as Ronald Knox so carefully pointed out, what would Stampede, who never had any stage experience, know about makeup?"

"The poor man must be mad."

"Mad enough to kill with a gun, not the more subtle weapons available to saner men who resent women. But his resentment was easily recognizable to any academic woman with feminist leanings. You should never have left the world of higher education, my dear Mariana, if you wanted to know all there was to know about motives for murdering aging or uppity women.

"Are you or are you not going to offer me a drink?"

THE PROPOSITION

On that particular evening, when Professor Kate Fansler settled at her desk to cope with the day's mail—those letters that had arrived at home and those she had carried back from her office—she first sorted through the stack, committing to the wastebasket those envelopes that declared themselves to be requests for funds whether commercial or charitable, and those with less than first-class postage. This left considerably fewer to be examined with suspicion and sighs. The truth was, most of Kate's mail, however first-class the postage, consisted of demands for recommendations, tenure reviews, contributions (literary, not financial), and the occasional request for a book review.

Today's mail offered only one envelope not immediately identifiable: from Texas, a town called Litany—yes, Litany; Kate examined the return address and the postmark with care—and carrying the message "Postman, please forward if necessary and possible." Forwarding had turned out to be neither necessary nor possible, but, on the other hand, the letter had to have been intended for someone else. Even Kate's most distant students, teaching in odd colleges in odder places, had never achieved so unlikely an address as Litany, Texas. From whom could such a letter be, and for whom? Kate doubted that, in reaching her, it had reached its intended destination. "Open it, for God's sake," Reed had he been there would have demanded in his most husbandly manner. But, left to her own devices, Kate hoped to solve the puzzle without, so to speak, sneaking a glance at the answer.

In the end, she had to give up and slice open the envelope. Even so, when she had discovered the signature at the bottom of the page she was not immediately wiser. *Sr. Monica Robinson.* Kate, she was certain, knew no sisters in Texas, and no one named Monica. Kate was actually driven to reading the letter. "Dear Kate," it began:

"I TRUST THAT, after a moment's cogitation, you will remember me and our long talks into the night, although I was named Leslie then; I never liked the name though you, I recall, did. I'm now Monica, and still the one who believed in God while you, I vividly remember, were the one convinced that the only true Christians you had ever met were humanists; you would have said 'secular humanists' had the term yet come into fashion. Certainly you had much reason and sound argument on your side. The harm, the cruelty, the suffering inflicted in the name of Christ is no easier to defend now than it ever was. Were we to meet today (which is what I hope for), and were we to pick up our ancient controversy (which I scarcely dare to hope for), you would no doubt take a more tolerant but no less firm

stand in defense of a godless if not lawless universe. I wish
we could have the discussions now as we had them when
we were young and tactless and wonderfully earnest.

"But I must not go on as though we had all the time in
the world, as we did in our youth. I write because I need
your help and hope I may ask you for it, plainly and
without excuse, on the basis of our long-ago friendship and
what I remember as your generosity, called humanist by
you but recognized as a kind of holiness by me. (I realize
this sounds like flattery, and may offend you; believe me, I
mean exactly what I say.)

"But to my point. I live here in Litany with a small group
of sisters who serve the rather bleak Texas communities for
miles around. We perform many of the services the
Church insists must rightly be performed by priests, by
men properly ordained. But there are few enough of those
about, and the number dwindles by the month. We live in
a house built not long ago for his Church by a man who
was born in these parts; it is adobe-like, with white stucco
walls, and must have been quite beautiful at one time. We
sisters still find it strangely peaceful and attractive too,
though it is run down and worn down by the constant
winds and dust. It is lonely, even desolate country hereabouts in the High Plains, where few stay if they can find a
way to go. Yet some of us love it with a passion as intense
as it is inexplicable. I feel sure, dear Kate, that you will not
understand that passion, but I ask you to visit in the hope
of your offering temporary help, not of my converting you
to my strange tastes in religion and landscape. In fact, I can
offer you nothing except my gratitude and my blessing,
whether or not you value it.

"But I have not yet reached the point; you must by now
doubt that I shall ever reach it. Here it is: we had here, in

our possession, I might admit as our prized possession, a painting by a seventeenth-century woman artist named Judith Leyster. Perhaps you will have heard of her. I never had, but I now know, as do we all, a certain amount about her. If you happen to own or have access to a history of women painters by Ann Sutherland Harris and Linda Nochlin and read about Judith Leyster therein, you will know all I know about that artist.

"Our painting was, we were told, a rather inferior reproduction, but for all that none the less valued by us. It is called 'The Proposition,' and seemed to many an odd painting for a convent. But it is the picture of an honorable woman refusing money for sexual favors, and is, according to Harris and Nochlin, the only portrayal in that genre of a firm refusal; in every other example of such pictures the proposition was accepted if the money was sufficient. That Leyster was the only woman painting in that genre is no doubt significant.

"Someone, dear Kate, has stolen our painting. But why? And what, in this barren place, could they dream of doing with it? It is not hidden anywhere in Litany nor in any town within many miles of Litany: we have ascertained that, and you must believe me. No one has left the area recently enough to be accused of having taken our picture with them. We stare at the empty place on our wall and miss our picture terribly, I more terribly than any of the others.

"Please, dear Kate, come and help us to recover our picture. That is the point of this long letter.

"I add only one further personal note. The picture came here as the gift of a woman who joined our order some years ago. She was not from these parts, and I don't know how she came to be here, except that God moves in mysterious ways, to say nothing of the Church hierarchy. She was a woman I came to love, Kate. She is dead, and the picture was her legacy to me and to the other sisters, but especially to me. I want to recover it. I hope you will take some satisfaction in proving that humanistic detection can accomplish what God and prayers cannot. Or perhaps you are the answer to my prayer.

"Please come, dear Kate, for my sake and for the sake of our youthful friendship."

TOUCHING AS THE letter was, Kate would no doubt have responded with a regretful refusal had she not, by coincidence or the hand of God depending on your point of view, been scheduled to visit Dallas the next week. A call the next day to her travel agent revealed that it was quite possible to fly from Dallas–Fort Worth to Amarillo, the airport nearest to Litany; indeed, the agent surprisingly informed Kate, the Amarillo airport had the second-longest runway in the United States. "That's comforting," Kate said. "Is there a reason?" The reason, hardly comforting, was that the runway had been built to launch nuclear warheads assembled in Amarillo. The warheads were now being disassembled, or something like that, the travel agent cheerfully added. "Watch out for plutonium," she had said, signing off.

Kate's only other preparation, apart from writing Sister Monica with her plans, was to consult the Harris-Nochlin book Sister Monica had mentioned.* "The Proposition" was there, with the comment Sister Monica had referred to: "While paintings and prints showing men making indecent proposals to women were common in the Low Countries in the sixteenth and seventeenth centuries, a work portraying

---

*Ann Sutherland Harris and Linda Nochlin, *Women Artists 1550–1950* (New York: Alfred A. Knopf, 1977).

a woman who has clearly not invited such an invitation and refuses to accept it is unique." There was a color plate of the beautiful and unusual painting. It brought to mind, in the light of Anita Hill and the growing concern with sexual harassment, all the women who had had, without complaint, to fend off for so many years such unwelcome invitations.

By the time Kate arrived in Amarillo, having given her talk in Dallas, she began to wonder if, unlike the lady in Leyster's picture, she had acquiesced too easily in what was, after all, an outrageous proposition. Her worries were increased by the fact that the plane did not go immediately into reverse upon landing, as most planes on shorter runways, certainly on all New York runways, were forced to do. Having automatically braced herself for the jolt as the pilot went into reverse, she had the sensation of some failure, of the certainty that they would smash into something. But they glided to a smooth stop and taxied toward the airport building. Sister Monica, as Kate must learn to call her, was waiting. She was dressed as a nun, not with a wimple but with a handkerchief over her hair and a dress and skirt that were clearly part of a uniform. Suddenly, Kate felt shy and wondered again why on earth she had come.

But Sister Monica was warmth itself, taking Kate's bag and leading her to the car, all the while expressing her gratitude. "The convent is not too far as distance is reckoned in these parts," she said. "I thought we might take the scenic route."

Looking with amazement from the car window, Kate wondered what the nonscenic route could possibly be like. Except for the very occasional tree, slight ups and downs on the road, a few curves, there was nothing scenic: all was fields, or plains, or prairie, or whatever they called it, with swirling dust and other evidence of wind. "The wind is not too bad this time of year," Sister Monica said. "Other months, it can blow you off the road."

Kate could not imagine that one might choose to live in such a place. But Sister Monica, questioned, said that she had chosen to come here, that she loved this country. Suddenly Kate thought of Alexandra, in Willa Cather's novel *O Pioneers!*: "For the first time, perhaps, since that land emerged from the waters of geologic ages, a human face was set toward it with love and yearning." Kate doubted that Sister Monica was, like Alexandra, the first to look on this land with love, but there could not, Kate thought, have been many others. Apart from ranchers and builders of nuclear warheads, why had anyone chosen to come here? Perhaps the sisters found God more accessible in this bleak place.

"There's been a new wrinkle since we last spoke," Sister Monica said. "For a time it looked as though the priest had taken the picture."

"What priest?" Kate asked.

"They come on their rounds, the few priests left in these parts, to hear confessions and give absolution. There are fewer and fewer priests, and those that are here are hardworking."

"That hardly explains one stealing a painting."

"Well," Sister Monica said, saluting a lone tree as she passed it, "he has long been fascinated with the picture; his fascination took the form of his insisting on its inappropriateness for a company of religious women. We, of course, considered it a highly religious painting. The argument has been going on for years. But now the sisters are wondering if the priest may not have taken matters into his own hands."

"You can hardly expect me to get it back from him," Kate said with asperity. She was tired, and felt on a fool's mission. Reed, who had tried to dissuade her, was certainly right. She ought to listen to him more, and not to her strange impulses on behalf of old acquaintances.

"It wasn't him," Sister Monica said. "That turned out to be a mare's nest. I'll spare you the details. The mystery is as deep as ever. Ah, here we are."

"Here" turned out to resemble not only an adobe but Kate's idea of an adobe, which was surprising of it. Sister Monica showed Kate to the guest room, cell-like as befitted a convent, but with its own bath, for which Kate thanked whatever gods there be. Later Kate met the other sisters, including the one in charge of the convent, and was soon led to the place where the picture had been. It had hung in the refectory, in the middle of the longest wall on one side of the oblong hall. The wall opposite was filled with windows looking out on a courtyard—windows admitting light, but gazing away from the world.

Kate studied the now empty wall with some puzzlement. "How big was the picture?" she asked.

Small, they told her: about a foot high and three-quarters of a foot wide. Kate was amazed. The color plate in the book had somehow given her the impression of a large painting—inevitable, of course, with one color plate to a page, each reproduced to the same size.

"No doubt someone simply cut out the canvas and rolled it up, perhaps during the night," Kate said. "It would fit nicely up a sleeve or under a long skirt. Anyone could have taken it."

"It wasn't a canvas," Sister Monica said. "I should have mentioned that. The picture had been painted on a wooden panel. And while it was small for so impressive a picture, it was rather too large to conceal even under the fullest skirt. No, it had to be taken away directly when it was removed from the wall. There wasn't even any likely hiding place for it; what places there are have been thoroughly searched, I promise you."

"Are there any other facts you've omitted?" Kate asked, rather more sharply than she intended. "Anything else I ought to know," she added in kinder tones.

But Sister Monica was not offended, only interested in answering the question fully. "There is only one other fact that interests me," she said, "but I'm sure it can't have anything to do with our problem. Judith Leyster was unique in another way: she was the only woman artist whose father had not been an artist. He was, in fact, a brewer."

"Well, that's interesting, if not exactly helpful under the circumstances," Kate said, smiling. "I'll think I'll turn in for now. As they used to say in the fairy stories, 'morning is wiser than evening.' "

THE NEXT DAY Kate asked to be taken on a tour of the region, but nothing indicative of art theft appeared. Kate could now well understand that a stolen picture could hardly be hidden anywhere about. The sisters were in and out of houses, they talked to everyone, Catholic or not, they knew all their neighbors. That one of these should suddenly have turned into a kleptomaniac or an art thief was beyond belief. The picture had been stolen, as all such pictures are stolen, either to be treasured in secret by some rich misanthropic collector for whom possession was its own, and the only, reward, or to be held for ransom.

"It's always been difficult to understand the theft of famous paintings," Kate said, as she and Sister Monica rode along. "They can't be sold; one can't even admit possession of them, as with a kidnapped person."

"What usually happens?" Sister Monica asked. "Do the pictures eventually turn up?"

"Mostly they do, I think," Kate said. "They're dumped somewhere, and returned to the museum—it's usually a museum—whence they came. But there are some mysteries remaining. The most recent theft, at least that I know of, was from the Isabella Stewart Gardner Museum in Boston. Their Vermeer, 'The Concert,' an immensely valuable painting, was simply gone one morning when the curators came in, along with several other paintings, I think. The mystery has yet to be solved. The favorite guess is that it was given as ransom in some drug deal, but don't ask me how that works exactly. I suppose there is always an underground market for famous paintings. And Vermeer is particularly valuable because he painted so few."

Kate was glad to renew her friendship with Sister Monica, and found the few days spent with her strangely rewarding. They agreed now, as in their youth, on practically nothing. Sister Monica had, however, a lasting affection for Kate, and Kate found that she felt profound respect, not easily accounted for, toward Sister Monica. No decision in Sister Monica's life seemed comprehensible to Kate; nor could Kate understand for a minute why anyone would want to live in this desolate, windswept place. And yet, she had not a moment's doubt that Sister Monica's commitment was sincere and heartfelt. Kate wished she could help her to get her painting back.

But after some peaceful, refreshing days in the sisters' adobe home, Kate returned to New York having failed in her mission.

YET EVEN AS Kate took up her wholly different, far more harried life in New York City, the problem of the vanished Judith Leyster painting would not fade away. She found herself reading books on art and art collectors that she would never before have found intriguing. It was one of these books that first gave Kate the glimmer of an idea.

Being a New Yorker she did not, with Sister Monica's sweet patience, sit down and write a letter. She immediately grabbed the telephone and demanded of the startled Texas operator the number of the convent. After a certain number of false trails, Kate was given, by a mechanical voice, the number of the adobe house in Litany. Kate dialed it, and was answered by the mother superior or whatever she was, who curtly informed Kate that sisters could not be summoned to the telephone except in emergencies. Kate, slowing down, identified herself and explained what it was she wished to speak to Sister Monica about. Sister Monica, she was finally told, would be available to speak to "Miss" Fansler at seven that evening.

And so at nine, her time, Kate was able to question Sister Monica. "Tell me about the man who built the building for your order," Kate asked, she hoped not too peremptorily.

"I don't know much about him" came the answer. "He was born here, went away and grew rich. He wanted to do something for his birthplace, and built this building for the Church. In time, the priest who was then in charge in these parts gave it to our order, having nothing else to do with it. At least we have tried to keep it from collapsing entirely."

"Where is he now?"

"Who? The priest? He retired and has not been replaced."

"I meant the man who gave the building to the Church," Kate said. Be patient, she admonished herself, take it easy.

"I don't know where he is. Do you want me to try to find out?"

"If you can," Kate said. "Do you know his name?"

"Yes," said Sister Monica, giving it. "Why, Kate?"

"I'll tell you when I've followed out this idea, if it leads to anything. If it doesn't, there's no point. Just one more question, Monica—Sister Monica."

"Yes?"

"Would it be hard or easy for someone, a stranger, to steal the painting? I mean, are there times when no one is about, when, say, a car or a person coming or going might not be observed?"

"I suppose so," Sister Monica said. "One or more sisters are usually about. But we have so much to do, there are so many people who need us, that if someone were to watch and wait—yes, I suppose a car or person would not be observed. Everyone around here has a car; we have several. There's no other way to get about."

"Thank you," Kate said. "I'll be in touch. I'll write, in fact, since telephoning seems an intrusion. I'll either tell you what I think happened to your painting, or I'll tell you that I have not the least idea what happened to your painting; I'll write in either case."

"Good-bye, dear Kate," Sister Monica said. "God bless."

Kate, hanging up at her end, found herself pleased by the blessing. Odd, she thought.

THE DONOR OF Sister Monica's adobe convent was not hard to find. He was, indeed, famous in many circles, not least as an art collector. Kate found out a great deal about him—which took several months of intermittent questions by her and someone hired by her—including his recent travels and acquisitions. Certainly he was not known to have any painting by Judith Leyster, or indeed from that period. He specialized rather in French and Italian paintings.

In the end, Kate turned back to her books, back to

where she had begun: with Harris and Nochlin. She knew by now that "The Proposition" had been acquired by the Mauritshuis Museum in 1892 as the work of an unknown artist. No recent study of the painting had been published, at least by the date of the Harris-Nochlin book. It was while reading a book by Aline B. Saarinen sometime later that Kate solved the mystery. At least, she was able to tell Sister Monica where the painting was, but it was up to Sister Monica to get it back, or to request help from the authorities to get it back.

But Sister Monica retrieved the painting alone, by her own efforts. She found out where the donor of the sisters' building was living, and went to see him. What she said to him, how she managed, before that, to be shown into his presence, she told no one, then or later, not even Kate. Her gratitude to Kate was eagerly expressed: the sisters prayed for her and blessed her as they stood in the refectory, admiring their recovered painting, as mysteriously returned to them as it had been mysteriously abducted.

Sister Monica not only prayed for Kate, and blessed her, she wrote her to thank her more formally. "I wish there were some manner by which I could repay you," she wrote, "but I know such are not the ways of God. You honored our youthful friendship, and I shall always be grateful and marvelously moved by that. I know that friendship to you means something of what holiness means to me, and although you will not call your commitment from God, I am, of course, free to call it what I will. Was it God or you who led me to the picture, who arranged its return to us? I shall never know. And of course, dear Kate, if you do not care to tell me, I shall never know how you managed to guide me to the recovery of the painting, for which we are all eternally grateful."

•   •   •

KATE DID IN the end write to Sister Monica to explain what she had extrapolated from her reading. Kate did so because she felt she owed it to what Sister Monica no doubt thought of as her, Kate's, secular humanism. If God exists, and operates, and affects events, Kate—never one to abandon a debate—argued, He or She has to work through human beings, and therefore His or Her existence must remain forever in question.

"As for what I guessed, dear Sister Monica," Kate wrote, "it was inspired by an essay Aline Saarinen wrote on Isabella Stewart Gardner, whose Vermeer we spoke of, although that theft took place long after Saarinen's book.* Saarinen pointed out that Italian families, at the time of the great American art collectors like Isabella Stewart Gardner, hated selling their pictures, hated looking at bare places on their walls, hated admitting that they were in straitened circumstances: 'When these proud aristocrats sold paintings, they usually demanded a copy to serve as a permanent "stand-in." ' These ersatz pictures have 'created a certain amount of confusion in the art world,' Saarinen notes.

"Well, dear Monica, I put this information, which might, I thought, apply to others besides the Italians, together with the fact that when the Mauritshuis acquired your Leyster painting, they put it in the basement, since it was by an unknown painter. Sometime, who knows when, a copy—or so I suspect—was made and placed in the store-room. When women's paintings became more interesting to the art world, or perhaps earlier, 'The Proposition' moved up to a gallery. But was it the real painting, or an excellent copy made most carefully on an old wood panel of the same size, with paints that would have been available in the seventeenth century?

* Aline B. Saarinen, *The Proud Possessors: The Lives, Times and Tastes of Some Adventurous American Art Collectors* (New York: Random House, 1958).

"I suspected, in short, that your picture, dear Monica, had come under the eye of your rich benefactor, who believed it, not the one in the Dutch museum, to be the original, and who determined to acquire it. Whether he did, and how, only you know, and you are not telling. My guess—yet another guess—is that he meant to leave you with a reproduction, but either was unable to because of someone's unexpected return to the adobe, or decided against it in the belief that you would know the difference.

"Guard your painting well, Sister Monica. You might request insurance on it from your benefactor, who would no doubt be pleased to offer so appropriate a gift. I draw no conclusions about your Leyster painting, or about the identical one now in the Netherlands, but rest simply content to rejoice in the happy return of your property. The priest was wrong. It is entirely appropriate to the sisterhood that owns it.

With all good wishes,
Kate"

THE GEORGE ELIOT PLAY

Kate Fansler gazed at the candidate undergoing his Ph.D. oral certification examination with a steadiness that she hoped conveyed genuine interest in his theories about George Eliot. And, indeed, her interest was not feigned. This student, a highly talented young man, had chosen George Eliot as his major author and was discoursing upon her novels and the theories about them with grace and intelligence, revealing easy familiarity with Eliot and the major works of criticism she had inspired. He finished up with an elegant and short disquisition on Eliot's ideas of vocation, using a few well-chosen examples, and the chair of the committee signaled that the time allowed for that section of the examination had expired. Kate smiled at the candidate and thanked him, quite sincerely, for his presentation.

The next section of the examination was on the medieval love lyric, and while Kate would assign a grade to this as to all other sections of the exam, she allowed her mind to wander. The fact was that if the candidate had made up out of whole cloth every one of the love lyrics he quoted, Kate would not have known the difference. Besides, George Eliot reminded her of the strangest bit of detective work she had ever been called upon to do. The case had only recently wound its way to its odd conclusion.

KATE HAD BEEN sitting in her office reading through applications to the graduate program when there came a knock on her door. She had called "Come in" before she remembered her determination to get through this pile of applications without interruptions. A young woman entered the office, her hand still resting diffidently on the door handle.

"May I talk to you for a moment?" she asked.

"If it really is only a moment," Kate said. "I've got to finish up dealing with this." She pointed to the bundles of purple folders on her desk.

"Well," the girl said, as though honesty were the only possible answer in this and in all matters, "it is longer than a moment. But everyone I consulted said you would be the only person who might help. Not that I consulted many people," she added. "Only three, to be exact, but they all mentioned you."

"In what connection?" Kate could not resist asking.

"George Eliot," the young woman said.

"Ah," Kate answered. "What's your name?"

"Luellen Sampson. I have a Ph.D. in English literature from another university, not here, and I'm an assistant professor of literature." Which, Kate thought, explained nothing, except that the interruption would have better been directed to another professor, whose office was quite elsewhere.

"Could we make an appointment, Ms. Sampson?" Kate asked. "I really must get through this job." Again she pointed to her desk.

"Of course. You couldn't help me with only one meeting anyway. I don't know if you can help me at all. You see"– and here Luellen Sampson paused; even her body seemed to come to attention as though she were about to attempt a difficult dive, which, Kate later acknowledged, was indeed the case–"you see, I've found an unpublished play by George Eliot and her companion George Henry Lewes, but mostly by George Eliot, apart from the main plot. Lewes probably outlined that."

Kate put her pen, which she had been grasping with the air of one determined to return to her task despite all disruptions, down on the desk. She leaned back in her chair. "All right," she said. "Tell me."

"I'm afraid it's a long story."

"It can hardly help being a long story," Kate agreed. "Why not start from the beginning, that is, with George Eliot. What year are we in?"

"1863. A man named Theodore Martin, who was an old friend of Lewes's–they'd met before Lewes went to live with George Eliot as her husband, though not legally; of course her name was Marian Evans when she went to live with Lewes, she hadn't begun writing novels yet. . . ." Luellen paused as though unable to disentangle herself from that sentence.

"I know about George Eliot's life," Kate said, not unkindly. "I've even heard of Theodore Martin. Wasn't he married to a famous actress?"

"Oh, very good," Luellen burst out, as though Kate were a student she was encouraging. "That's the whole point, you see. He was married to an actress named Helen Faucit, whom Lewes thought the best tragic actress he'd ever seen, and since George Eliot was in one of her sad phases, he, Lewes, suggested that they write a play for Helen Faucit." Luellen paused; her sentences, Kate noticed, tended to become unduly extended although the elements of proper syntax were never quite abandoned. "They decided to call the play *Savello*," Luellen concluded with a sigh. "That's the play I've found."

Kate considered this statement in a deepening silence. The woman was probably demented, though not necessarily in a dangerous way. George Eliot materials had been searched out endlessly and thoroughly; the chance of anything else, certainly anything more than a letter, being found was unlikely to the point of impossibility. On the other hand, of course, a first novel of Louisa May Alcott's had just been discovered in, of all obscure places, the Houghton Library at Harvard, where it had been misfiled. And then there were Boswell's journals, which had surfaced more than seventy years ago, in a croquet box. All the same . . .

Luellen had risen to her feet. Kate rose also, to stretch her legs and to escort her visitor to the door. But Luellen was taking a large brown envelope from her backpack.

"Here," she said. "I'll leave you a copy. You can read it, and then we can talk about it. People said I could trust you, and there doesn't seem to be anyone I can trust any better. Can we make an appointment to meet after you've read it? No hurry."

Kate should have said that she hadn't the time, that she didn't want to be responsible for deciding what might become of a valuable, unknown manuscript, that this wasn't the sort of problem she could help with, or any of a hundred other things. Instead, her hand, as though with a mind of its own, reached out and took the brown envelope.

"Come back on Monday, this time. Is that convenient? I'll read this over the weekend and we can confer on Monday."

"Fine," Luellen said. "And thank you. I know you won't show it to anyone or discuss it with anyone." And she departed with more alacrity than Kate would have given her credit for.

To Kate, the "anyone" she was not supposed to discuss "it" with did not include Reed, and at dinner she told him about Luellen's visit and about the play that the young woman intended to publish, making her reputation and–so Luellen clearly assumed–her academic fortune. Kate had read the play after her return home and before Reed, who had been kept late by a meeting, joined her for a drink and dinner.

"What's the play about?" Reed asked, when he had heard an account of Kate's afternoon meeting with Luellen Sampson. "I know that's not the proper way to question a literary work. I guess I mean, what's the plot?"

"That's easier described than what the play's about," Kate said, laughing. "We have this Don Juan type, named Savello, who sees the beautiful Cassandra–and why they chose that name, only God and George Henry Lewes know, and they've both forgotten–anyway, he sees her in church, naturally, shades of Dante, and desires her, or lusts after her, whatever."

"You usually describe literary works more elegantly, Kate."

"This is scarcely a literary work. I'll try to be quick about the hideous plot. You can probably guess it for yourself. Savello follows her home and covers her with words and kisses, all gentle enough not to upset her unduly. In fact, instead of defending her virtue, she paints for him a picture of the hideous life he will live if he continues on his feckless way. Deciding she has saved his soul, he sends her a note saying he must see her one more time, he tricks her husband–I think I forgot to say she was married–"

"You certainly did," Reed interrupted.

"Yes, well, she is, but she tells her husband about Savello, and then tells Savello to come, which he does, and the husband kills him, or maybe Cassandra does—it's not terribly clear—but she is sobbing over his body; she now understands that he has indeed been ennobled by her love, but she has killed him before he could live his noble life. Curtain."

"Yikes!" Reed said.

"The perfect comment. But if George Eliot did write it, even with the help of Lewes, finding and publishing it is certainly worth a lot of academic credits."

"I'm afraid I don't quite get it," Reed said. "Why did she come to you, and what's the problem you're supposed to be coping with?"

"Good question," Kate said. "Go to the head of the class."

"What's the good answer?"

"Only a guess. I think she needed someone from outside her circle to lend a name to the play, back it, push it, blurb it, endorse it, certify its authenticity. I'm something of an expert in the field of the novel, and something of a detective. If I say George Eliot wrote it, then a number of people will assume that she did. And those who think she didn't will attack *me* as well as Luellen Sampson."

"Are you going to endorse it?"

"Really, Reed, of course I'm not. George Eliot never wrote that thing, and while there is evidence that her 'husband' wrote the plot or at least the outline, I don't think he had a hand in it either. It's not so much the language and the syntax, although that's not of the greatest. It's other signs. Commas, for one thing. George Eliot, like Jane Austen, had a view of comma use wholly different from what today's grammarians condone, and the commas in this play are, so to speak, modern."

"What about the paper and the type?"

"They've gone to a lot of trouble about that. I'm no expert, but I'd be surprised if both aren't exactly what John Blackwood, her publisher, would have used in 1863."

"I see," Reed said. "Well, supposing it is a fake, where did she, or whoever did it, get the idea for the play?"

"The same place where I learned about it, from Gordon Haight's biography of George Eliot,* a really great biography, even if he was somewhat overconvinced that 'she was not fitted to stand alone.' What I don't know is what, if anything, I'm going to do about it. Of course I'm not going to endorse it, but . . ."

"But," Reed finished the sentence for her, "you're damn well going to find out whose plot this was and why they decided to involve you in it?"

"Exactly. Still, easier said than done. I'll have to do a bit of digging."

"Starting with Luellen Sampson, assistant professor of literature?"

"However did you guess?" Kate said, smiling at him. But her days were full for the rest of the week, and the weekend too had long since been promised to other activities. And so it was that Kate saw Luellen again before she could begin any of her investigations.

LUELLEN ARRIVED EXACTLY as she had before, knocking and then entering with an apologetic air, if one could be imagined, Kate thought, to offer apologies for what one was nonetheless determined upon. Invited to sit, Luellen did so.

*Gordon S. Haight, *George Eliot: A Biography* (Oxford: Oxford University Press, 1968).

"I've read the play," Kate said. "If it wasn't by George Eliot, I doubt anyone would find it of great interest. Do you agree?"

"Well, I hadn't thought of it like that," Luellen said, startled by the question. "I mean, since it is by George Eliot, it's very interesting indeed."

"From a biographical point of view, I guess so," Kate said. "I for one have never been able to get my pulses racing over Eliot's *The Spanish Gypsy*, and this is more or less in that mode, isn't it?"

"Well, yes. It's verse, and it's got a very serious moral point to make. Still, one might not have guessed at what George Eliot's views would be on a Don Giovanni type."

This discussion, intriguing to anyone for whom literature was the stuff of life, had to be postponed.

"Tell me about yourself," Kate said, "with an emphasis on your graduate school experience, unless something dramatic happened before then."

"Yes," Luellen said, "I thought you'd want to know about me. That's only natural. There was nothing whatever dramatic in my life until I got to college. Then I met a man, really the first man who ever paid serious attention to me, the first one who ever listened to what I had to say, and I married him just to have someone to listen to me. Only, after we were married . . ."

"He stopped listening," Kate provided, after a pause.

"Yes. He thought I was the docile type. Well, I was the docile type, I guess, and he thought I'd be the kind of wife he wanted. But I insisted on finishing college and even said I was going on to graduate school. I loved literature." She said it the way, in a long ago and more distant time, men used to say "I loved my country." Now what made me think of that? Kate wondered.

"And then," Kate added, "he left, you left. What came next?" For Luellen certainly seemed to need encouragement to continue her story.

"It was funny. When we were in college, we seemed to be equals. Then, once we were married, he was reading the newspaper or watching a ball game in the living room and I was in the kitchen. If you know what I mean?"

Kate nodded to show she knew.

"That's all. I guess you'd have to say I left. I had inherited some money from my grandfather, just like Samuel Richardson's Clarissa Harlowe"—she waited while Kate smiled her recognition of the similarity—"not that someone was threatening to rape me. Anyway, I enrolled in graduate school and—"

"Let's go a little more slowly now," Kate said. "Did you get to know many students there? Were there any special professors you admired?"

"Benjamin Franklin was my mentor," she said. "I know it's an awfully funny name to have, but he signs himself B. Franklin, and everyone calls him Frank."

"I know who he is," Kate said. "That is, I've heard of him, naturally. He's a well-known critic of nineteenth-century novelists. *And* he's done some important work on George Eliot."

"Yes. I guess that's why I decided to write my dissertation on her. But I never thought I'd find this play and be able to edit it for publication. I hope it will get me tenure. It should, don't you think?"

"How close was your relationship with B. Franklin? And if you think I'm suggesting something untoward, I may be."

"You don't believe in sex between people who love each other?"

"I don't believe in sex between a professor and a

student, or between a person in power and a person dependent on that power, no. Some lasting marriages have come out of such affairs, but not many, and not when the professor is married to someone else at the time. Was B. Franklin married?"

Luellen blushed. "Yes," she said. "He was. I did feel guilty about that, but, well, I couldn't really help myself."

"And did he listen to you, at least at first?"

"Oh, no. I listened to him. But he did appreciate the fact that I could listen intelligently and ask meaningful questions. By this time, of course, he'd given up George Eliot and was writing on some less well-known male novelists. I loved discussing his work with him."

"His wife wasn't, on the other hand, able to ask such meaningful questions?"

"Oh, dear." Luellen dropped her head at Kate's tone, which, Kate knew, *had* been a bit harsh, and tried surreptitiously to wipe away a tear.

"What finally happened?" Kate asked. They had better stick to the relevant facts, or at least return to George Eliot.

"He found another student to ask meaningful questions, I guess," Luellen said, sniffing ominously. "I'm sorry," she added, accepting a Kleenex from a box Kate pulled from a desk drawer where she kept them for student use when required. "Does all this have anything to do with the play?"

"I don't know," Kate said. "It might. Tell me how you found the play. Did Frank help with that too?"

"Yes. Someone else had found it. It's a long story. Descendants of Helen Faucit's found it in an old box in the attic. Apparently George Eliot had given it to her when they decided not to publish it, and it just stayed there, in the same house."

"Which has been in the family all these years?"

"Oh, yes. Faucit and Theodore Martin moved to the country, to Surrey, and a niece of hers inherited the house, and it's stayed in the family, or branches of the family, ever since. They cleaned out the attic—well, it is like all those old stories about finding papers, but in this case it's true."

"And how did the play come into your hands?"

"I got a letter from the man who now owns the house, the one who had gone through the stuff in the attic when they decided to turn the attic into living quarters, and I went to England to look at what he'd found. He said he had been given my name by a friend who taught English in a school and was crazy about George Eliot. The friend had read my dissertation; it was about George Eliot's conviction of the necessity of work. I was surprised that he'd even heard of it, but life is like that sometimes."

"So you flew to England."

"I went right away. It was terribly exciting. The schoolteacher didn't know what to make of it, but he agreed that it seemed likely to be a play by her; it had all her seriousness and rather shaky verse."

"Great ideas, but better expressed in prose."

"Exactly." Luellen nodded her agreement.

"And you brought the play back and asked for Frank's advice." It wasn't exactly a question. "Surely the authentication would have been easier if the play had been handwritten, either by Eliot or by Lewes; there are plenty of examples of their handwriting around for comparison. Didn't you think it odd that it was set in type if it was never to be published?"

"It wasn't so surprising. When Eliot was struggling with *The Spanish Gypsy* her publisher Blackwood offered to set it into type for her so that she could correct it more easily, and he did. He probably made the same offer in this case, but when she saw the play in type she abandoned it."

"Wisely, don't you think?" Kate asked.

"Probably, from her point of view. But from our point of view as students of her life and work, it's of great interest. Surely you can see that?"

"I certainly read it with interest," Kate admitted. "I might even say I was riveted by it. Surely the expectation of a beautiful woman's reforming a rake had been seen to be highly unlikely even in Eliot's time—once a rake, always a rake. In fact, Eliot was remarkably astute in recognizing the tendency of people to follow their dominant trait to the end, wouldn't you agree?"

"Well, as I said in my dissertation, quoting Mr. Farebrother from *Middlemarch*, 'if a man is denied love from one woman he can eventually obtain it from another, but not so with one's work: there is a fit, a suitability, a properness which, once botched, can never be made good.' I think maybe Eliot came to see that this isn't true. After all, Lydgate in *Middlemarch* marries the wrong woman—which botches his work; Farebrother probably was consoling himself for losing Mary Garth."

"But," Kate said, "you notice that we are discussing *Middlemarch* and not *Savello*. What, after all, is there to discuss about that dreary play?"

"I don't think that matters," Luellen said, with more audacity and confidence than she had shown before. "It's by George Eliot, and that makes it both valuable and interesting apart from its inherent defects."

"George Eliot would probably not want you to publish it," Kate said.

Luellen shrugged. There was no real answer to that. What George Eliot would have thought of most of the criticism her works had inspired was anybody's guess, but her opinion did not matter in the least. In any case, criticism is dissolved by time, but literature remains.

"What, then, do you want from me?" Kate asked. "Beyond my reading the play and talking to you about it?"

"I hoped you'd write an introduction to it. That would give it cachet and get it noticed by the right people. I do want something more than an article in the newspapers. I don't mind if you say you think it's a lousy play. After all, George Eliot did decide not to publish it. But you might suggest why the plot would have appealed to her in the first place."

"Perhaps it only appealed to Lewes, and she went along for his sake."

"But he had obviously thought it up because he believed that writing it would help her. You could discuss all that, and anything else that intrigued you. You'd get an honorarium of course, and some of the royalties. I'd like to make this splash in the company of a critic I admire, a woman critic. I've about decided that men don't really understand Eliot; not even Haight understands her altogether."

"Let me think about it," Kate said. "I'll call you when I've decided."

And so Luellen left her telephone number with Kate and went away.

ALTHOUGH KATE, BY this stage in her academic career, had acquaintances on many campuses around the country, the university where B. Franklin worked included none of them. Kate had long been aware of Franklin as a critic of Victorian literature, but a quick scroll through the library computer revealed no recent publication of his, certainly nothing on male Victorian novelists. His last work, on George Eliot, had appeared twelve years ago. Perhaps he had been writing articles not yet gathered between book covers, but the search for these, while requiring the help of a reference librarian, and a student of Kate's who happened to run into her in the library, revealed nothing. Was that odd or wasn't it? Some professors, though happily not too many, having gained tenure, ceased to produce. Of these, some were hard-working members of their university community and highly competent teachers; others, alas, had simply dwindled into sloth.

Kate abandoned Franklin and went in search of Luellen Sampson's dissertation on George Eliot's idea of work. Although not published, hers, like all dissertations, was on microfilm and available. Kate arranged to have it sent to her, not on microfilm, which was hideous to read, but bound in a small volume.

None of this really satisfied her. It would have been obvious to anyone involved in whatever scheme was under way that she would check out the major players in exactly this way; their tracks must have been otherwise covered. Furthermore, she had no doubt that an expensive search in England, undertaken by a private investigator she knew there, would establish the reality of the house where the descendants of Helen Faucit lived, their decision to remodel the attic, and permission given to someone for the papers in the attic to be examined by a scholar. Nor, as she had told Reed, did she doubt that the paper and the type on which the play was written would prove to be the right paper and right type for 1863.

By paying for Federal Express and pleading for special favors, Kate got the dissertation within a week. Franklin was listed as the sponsor, with a number of other signatures appended. Kate settled down to read it with appreciation.

The dissertation was carefully argued and well-written; it was also decidedly familiar, yet Kate could not quite pin down what made it seem so familiar. That problem gnawed at her as the days went by. Still unable to solve the puzzle, she called Luellen to suggest another meeting about peripheral matters, saying she had not yet made a decision. Luellen, though with evident reluctance, agreed.

"I NEED A few more details," Kate said, when Luellen had sat down in Kate's office. "You said you wanted me to write an introduction. What exactly did you intend to contribute to the book, in addition to the play itself?"

"Well, nothing," Luellen said. "I was going to tell you that. In fact, it wasn't really me who found the play. That was an untruth, but I had, that is, I needed . . . I didn't see how I could approach you if I wasn't talking about my own project."

"B. Franklin found the play, is that it?" Kate asked.

"Well, yes. I suppose my story about an English teacher having heard of me wasn't very convincing. But of course he had heard of B. Franklin, and called him. The rest was all true, I swear."

"So I am to write an introduction to a book of B. Franklin's?"

"Well, yes." It was, Kate thought, to Luellen's credit that she made that admission concisely.

"Why didn't he talk to me himself?" Kate asked.

"Well, he knew your reputation as a feminist, and I guess he thought that you would be likelier to do a favor for a younger woman."

"But surely he would have to surface sooner or later and I would know I wasn't doing the favor for a younger woman."

Luellen looked unhappy. "I guess he hoped that that revelation would occur only after the book was so far along that you wouldn't refuse to continue. And after all, it is exciting to have a play by George Eliot, isn't it? It's a project anyone would be glad to be connected with, isn't it?"

Kate gazed at Luellen steadily, until the woman dropped her eyes. "I'll still have to think about it," Kate said. "I'll be in touch." And Luellen had no choice but to depart, even had she been able to think of anything else to say, which Kate strongly doubted.

SHE OUTLINED THE situation to Reed that night.

"I'd been wondering what happened to that Don Juan type," he said. "Have you decided to blow the gaff? Are you going to take Luellen to task for suggesting that George Eliot could write such a poor play?"

"Reed, do you know someone who could do a bit of academic sleuthing for me? I need to know more about B. Franklin and I don't want to be the one to ask, or even the one to ask someone else to ask."

"There's a law student in my clinic at the moment who was obviously born to be a detective. He uncovered something . . . well, I'll leave that for another time. What do you want him to do?"

"Go to Franklin's university, to Franklin's department. Mosey around, ask questions, pretend to be a someone planning to enroll there, whatever sounds workable. I want to know the gossip, as much of the truth as he can uncover, and Franklin's present status and situation. Is that possible?"

"We can but try. I gather I'm not to say it's for you; I'll think up some explanation. And upon our man's return, you'll tell me all?"

"More than you'll want to hear. Before I'm halfway done, you'll be saying, 'How about sending out for some Chinese food?' "

"It's a bargain."

SOME DAYS LATER Reed came home with the report from what he had taken to calling "the Franklin undercover operation." He threw himself onto the couch and demanded that Kate provide them both with a drink before he would utter so much as a syllable. She plied him with an excellent single malt Scotch and announced that she was waiting with bated breath.

"How does breath become bated?" Reed maddeningly asked. Kate reached over and grabbed his Scotch.

"All right," he said, taking it back. "I'm only stalling because I'm sure the report is exactly what you expected, probably in every detail. B. Franklin hasn't produced anything in years; he toils not, neither does he spin. I gather he's been spending most of his time alternating between prescription drugs and drink. It didn't take very long to find all of this out. But, together with his lack of publication and collegiality, he's missed enough classes so that there's been some move to try and get him out, either through retirement or by sterner measures. He has in the last months straightened up a bit and is even talking about publishing something. That something is still a great secret in his department, but you and I can guess what it is."

"Yes," Kate said, "I rather thought that was how it would be. Furthermore, he was a very clever writer before he started slipping down the drain, certainly clever enough to forge that George Eliot play, especially since she wasn't very good at verse plays *and* he had a model in *The Spanish*

Gypsy. Besides, all the really awful lines could be attributed to poor George Henry Lewes. But he had to launch it properly, if his new reputation was to be made. Perhaps he was really clever, and planted some slight suggestion in a preface of possible forgery to which he could point if and when the band began to play."

"But why involve you? Well, I can answer that: he wanted a foreword by a recognized critic to lend verisimilitude. But why not ask you himself? Why involve Luellen Sampson?"

"Men like Franklin never really understand women, and women who have a reputation for being feminist least of all. He no doubt considered that I couldn't resist such a request from a young woman making her way. I must say, she did put on a good act. He also counted on the fact that once I'd written the introduction I wouldn't be likely to let it go to waste just because the other person in the bargain changed identity. He assumed, quite rightly, that no academic lets any serious piece of writing go unpublished. And how else might I publish it but in his book?"

"Good answer," Reed said. "I like the way you work it all out. But the real mystery is still unsolved: Why did Luellen Sampson lend herself to this shoddy scheme? Is she in love with him? Has he promised her unknown goodies as reward? Or has he a hold on her?"

"Oh, yes, he has a hold all right," Kate said. "She didn't write her dissertation; she plagiarized it. Franklin was probably too strung out at the time to even bother reading it with care, but eventually the penny dropped. He decided not to 'out' her, as they say today, but to make use of her. At least, that's the way I think it went."

"You mean she didn't tell you?"

"Oh, no. You see, she quoted a speech from *Middlemarch*

to me, a speech from her dissertation. And somehow, it didn't sound quite right. I spent more time than I care to admit leafing through the novel until I realized the speech wasn't there at all. The words belonged to someone writing about Mr. Farebrother and, lo and behold, she had altered one word in that. She had changed the word 'vocation' to 'one's work.' She didn't want to use the word 'vocation' because that is in the title of the book she plagiarized: *George Eliot and the Novel of Vocation* by a man named Alan Mintz. The words she quoted were his, not Mr. Farebrother's. Mintz's book was published by the Harvard University Press in 1978, when Luellen was still in school. She no doubt stole it from the library and trusted that no one would remember the book."

"But you remembered it?"

"Eventually, yes. It was a good book. And as you know, the whole question of vocation has always intrigued me. Alas, poor Luellen thought she had a vocation for literary criticism but, like some other graduate students, she only had an affection for literature. As Mintz points out, Adam Bede's work as a carpenter is good because it produces objects 'that are the direct result of his own labor.' Poor Luellen failed that definition of vocation. The very essence of vocation is that it can't be had by cheating."

"You seem rather sanguine about this whole thing. Are you going to let it go with a polite refusal to write the introduction?"

"I rather think so. I was damn pissed at first. But, truthfully, I can't wait to see whether or not Franklin actually goes through with his plan to publish the play. And besides, I've begun to suspect that there was a bit more to the relationship between Franklin and Luellen than she has let on. I mean, I've come to suspect that my function in this whole stupid plot, even if I didn't write the introduction, was to get

rid of Luellen for him. He doesn't want to have to decide
on her tenure and all the rest of it. He hoped that I'd get rid
of her for him by exposing her plagiarism and getting her
struck from the rolls. Well, if he's got himself in a mess with
her, as I suspect, I'm going to let him stew in it."

"So you're not going to 'out' Luellen?"

"She knows she's published a dissertation she didn't
write. I can't rescue her from that, and I don't think she
needs any reprimands from me. And I bitterly resent
having my feminist sympathies manipulated in so corrupt
a way. Oh, the hell with it!"

"Good," Reed said. "How about sending out for some
Chinese food?"

GUILTILY, KATE RETURNED her attention to the young
man being examined, still making his way through the
medieval love lyrics. He was quoting one that Kate
was happy to discover she had long known and loved—
anonymous, of course, and therefore, as Virginia Woolf
had said, probably written by a woman. This one, at
least, he could not have fooled her by making up:

> Western Wind, when will thou blow,
>   The small rain down can rain?
> Christ, that my love were in my arms,
>   And I in my bed again!

A good student, gaining confidence as he made his way
through an excellent exam. He was unlikely to fall into the
snares that had entrapped B. Franklin and Luellen
Sampson. But who could tell? What, Kate wondered, can
one ever tell about these promising young people?

THE BARONESS

⌒◠◠◠◡◞

The invitation to dinner at
the House of Lords was startling enough, and the more so
in that the Baroness knew perfectly well I was in New York
City and would have to make my way to Parliament and
the Peers' Entrance at considerable expense and effort.
True, she had no reason to doubt that I could afford both
the time and the money, but that hardly served to mini-
mize my astonishment. Phyllida–though I liked, since her
elevation, to call her My Lady, exhibiting an American's
scorn for British titles–must have had something very
serious on her mind, the more so since she had been in
New York not many weeks before, and we had met then,
although for a shorter visit than we usually allowed ourselves: Phyllida was on some sort of business visit and had
almost to do a turnabout. She well understood–I had
known her through five decades–that I would come at
even a moment's notice if summoned by her. As it happened, being essentially old-fashioned in the best sense–

that is, regarding electronics and not morals—she had written a short letter and sent it by ordinary post. (I can never convince Phyllida how unreliable New York mail is; I shudder to think the letter might never have arrived.)

She had written simply enough, in her pleasant, legible hand:

"My dearest Anne,

"Please come to dinner at the House of Lords in a month, about a fortnight after you are likely to receive this letter. I must talk to you, and somehow the terrace at the House of Lords seems the place. (I shall also offer you dinner, though the food, I warn you, is quite uninspired. But I seem to remember that you always liked what you call 'plain English food.' You will get it.) Do not disappoint me. I shall await you at six-thirty [and she gave the date] at the Peers' Entrance. If you cannot come, a message can be left for me at . . ."

Dear, dear Phyllida. Her extraordinary tact had only matured, like wine, with the years. She knew that a letter left me time to think and to refuse if I had to; she knew that a more direct message would, were refusal necessary, have required immediate personal explanations and apologies. Phyllida, my dearest friend.

Of course I went—was, if truth be told, glad to go. I lead an extraordinarily pleasant life, but a sudden summons is exactly what it needs from time to time for spice and the right amount of excitement. One does not want too much excitement in one's sixties; certainly I don't. On the other hand, the occasional adventure, if sufficiently benign, is not to be lightly shunned. The question of how benign this adventure would be was one I determined not to engage with.

· · ·

I WAS EARLY at the Peers' Entrance, partly because–since England was having one of its regular railroad strikes, thus putting extra pressure on London taxis–I had left more than ample time, and partly because I rather anticipated having, if early, a chance to look around. I found I could not imagine what the Peers' Entrance or, for that matter, the House of Lords would be like; the House of Commons, through films and television news, was a far more familiar ambience.

I was early, as it turned out, and watched the lords come and go, all smoking, all assertively male, all moving under the watchful eye of a man in white tie and stiff shirtfront, with a large round medallion hanging round his neck. Sitting there, I contemplated England, which I had left–permanently, however often I visited–at the age of twenty. Phyllida and I, friends since the age of ten, had married brothers; mine had immediately decamped with me for the United States. Both brothers had been obsessed by flying since boyhood, but hers, remaining in England, had managed fatally to crash himself and his plane some ten years after my departure, leaving her with children to support and no professional preparation for supporting them. My husband, although he too remained enamored of planes, had gone to work in a small airfield and ended up owning both the field and an airline or two. I was a wife and mother, as they used to say before the women's movement, but both Phyllida and I had the usual English-woman's competence, then (and I suspect still) too often revealed only in the comfort and success of her husband.

Phyllida went to work for the government, eventually achieving one of those administrative positions that run the whole show and do not change with elections or parties. She became immensely valuable, if underpaid, and when, after the women's movement, they wanted one or two women on various important boards and such, she was appointed. Phyllida, as I never ceased to remind her, was a natural conservative and did not, therefore, flutter the dovecotes–that is to say, frighten the men. She was firm but gracious, ladylike and, more to the point, with a natural deference to the male and his need to dominate, or appear to dominate. We argued the point frequently, but Phyllida might have been said to have won when England showed its appreciation of her opinions and capabilities by making her a baroness.

I, eventually (but hardly soon enough), bored with my husband and no longer needed by my children, carved out my own life working for a law firm. What I became, in fact, was a kind of private detective, working on behalf of the lawyers in the firm who defended criminals, or those accused of crimes. Most of these clients were guilty, but that did not stop them or me from seeking out evidence that brought their guilt into question at the trial. I became very good at this.

Phyllida's and my children flew back and forth constantly to visit one another and became friends. Most of the flying was at my expense; I also used to help Phyllida out when circumstances grew tight. I will say for Phyllida that she did not make a fetish of taking money, recognizing perfectly well that had our situations been reversed, she would have expected me to be a courteous recipient. Besides, she agreed with me that a friendship such as ours deserved to be extended into the next generation.

Waiting just inside the House of Lords, and staring alternately at a television monitor reporting on the current debate or question before the house and, beyond the formal man in the white tie, at endless coatracks, I thought how nearly our situations had reversed themselves. Phyllida was now well off, and a prominent figure in many circles, a baroness, by God. I, with an interesting job devoid of status, and alimony (which I took gladly, feeling I deserved it after so many years advancing my husband's career) to pad my meager salary, was clearly the less exalted of us two.

PHYLLIDA GREETED ME with a modest hug that to anyone observing us would have seemed cool; we had never gone in for those dramatic embraces with which in the States even men greet each other these days. But the love I felt for her, and she for me, was—although Phyllida would never have dreamed of saying any such thing—stronger than family bonds. Not only sisters-in-law, Phyllida and I had each long been the chief member of the other's family.

When we were seated on the terrace, when, on the way there, I had admired the continuous red carpet (green for Commons, Phyllida told me), when the server had taken our order, when we had expressed our shared admiration for the Thames and answered each other's perfunctory questions about our children—perfunctory not because we did not care, but because we recognized that the children were not, this evening, our subject—only then, when we had raised our glasses, did Phyllida come to the point. That she came to it so directly—for Phyllida was a mistress of the indirect approach—bespoke her sense of urgency.

"The most awful thing has happened," she said.

"So I have somehow gathered. Whatever it is, Phyllida, knowing will be better than this suspense."

"You know the small Constable drawing that was stolen with the Vermeer a short time ago in New York, from that elegant small museum?"

I nodded, mystified. The theft had indeed been widely publicized, mainly because the main haul had been a Vermeer—there are only thirty-five or forty of them in the world—and no trace of it had been found. The robbers had taken, in addition, one other item, valuable, but not altogether beyond price as the Vermeer was. I had remembered about the drawing because it was by Constable, a favorite of mine, and with all the strange delicacy that an initial drawing may have that the finished painting, however magnificent, always lacks.

"Well"—Phyllida took a large sip of her drink and could be clearly seen to be gathering all her forces for the next announcement—"I have it," she said.

I admit that for one frightful moment I was simply worried about Phyllida, not because she had, it seemed, stolen a valuable drawing if not a Vermeer, but because she had gone mad—quietly mad, but mad nonetheless.

"Oh don't look at me as though you thought I'd grown a brain tumor," Phyllida said, annoyed.

"So you stole the Constable because we had always admired him even as girls," I snapped, cross at having my mind read. We used to joke, in school, that Turner, who painted fog, had produced endless pictures, but Constable, who painted English sunshine, had, inevitably, painted few.

"Of course not. As you know, I was exceedingly busy when I was last there—no time for even a small museum."

"I'm well aware of how busy you were," I said with some asperity. "Phyllida, for God's sake, what happened in New York? Someone gave you the drawing as a gift and you thought it was a reproduction?"

"Well, at last you're thinking about the problem," she said. "That's not true, but at least not insulting."

I determined to wait for further information before uttering another syllable.

"What I *think* happened is that the rolled-up paper was slipped into my bag, the one I carried on the plane with me, and of course no one examines luggage these days, at least they never examine mine. Yours?"

"No," I said. "But that's probably because—"

"Exactly. Old ladies with gray hair are hardly likely smugglers of stolen goods, or contraband, or drugs, or whatever does get smuggled these dreary days." Neither Phyllida nor I thought of ourselves as old, but we had faced the fact that so we appeared to the unperceptive multitudes.

"But if the thieves know that, why don't the customs people know it?"

"Because the thieves don't know. I think the whole horrible thing was a mistake—the wrong carry-on bag. Mine is rather ordinary and so, I can only suppose, resembled the one designed to receive the stolen drawing."

"How long have you had it?" I asked. I knew I had to get the facts, but my mind was mainly engaged with thinking of how the drawing might be returned with no one the wiser as to how or by whom. In this, as it soon transpired, I was, as is so often the case with us two, anticipating Phyllida. But she answered my question.

"Since I returned from New York, of course."

"Really, Phyllida."

"I know; spare me representations of my stupidity, I know them all. But the whole thing has been a shock. Later, I just about decided to call the authorities and simply tell them what happened, how it had been a mistake, how I didn't realize it was the actual drawing, how I was terribly sorry but had been frightfully busy, how I hoped that, since I am in the House of Lords, I would simply be believed when I turned it in. Then suddenly I realized with horror that because I *was* in the House of Lords, the whole scandalous matter would make a tasty headline in all the tabloids: BARONESS CLINGS TO STOLEN CONSTABLE FOR WEEKS. I got cold feet."

"Well, it was a good idea to turn it in," I said, "but I do see what you mean about the tabloids. There's something about women doing hanky-panky, especially baronesses and royalty, that seems to be irresistible to the gutter press. It's the same in the States."

Phyllida rose to her feet and waited until I had risen to mine. "Shall we go in to dinner? I'll tell you my plan." We were about to leave the terrace but stopped a moment for a last glimpse of the Thames in the setting sun. Suddenly, an extremely noisy motorboat shattered the air with its cacophony. "I don't steal art," Phyllida said between her teeth, "but I would very much like to throw a bomb at that boat. A quick explosion and the noise of the motor would cease; it might even frighten off others. Come on, then." I was suddenly back in our girlhood, when Phyllida would snap, "Come on, then" after keeping *me* waiting. I said nothing, but myself composed another tabloid headline: BARONESS BOMBS BOAT FROM HOUSE OF LORDS TERRACE.

Feeling rather anxious, as though I had learned that Phyllida had been diagnosed with something fatal and hideous, I followed her along the red carpet, watching her nod amiably to a few acquaintances, until we entered a smallish dining room ("Much better food than in the larger one," she muttered as we were led to a table) and the waitress greeted her with dignity and called her "my lady." The waitress smiled at me too, and I realized that I, who thought of myself as spectacularly out of place, probably resembled with alarming closeness most of the peers' wives who were taken from time to time to dine in this hallowed place; indeed, a few of them, I noticed, glancing around the room, were even now there.

. . .

"PHYLLIDA," I SAID when we had got to the Dover sole ("Of course not filleted," Phyllida told the waitress, "it tastes altogether different off the bones") and I was concentrating on lifting the meat neatly from the skeleton–one does not seem to eat Dover sole frequently in New York– "where exactly is the drawing now?"

"Here," she said.

"In this dining room?"

"The Lady Members' Cloakroom."

"Are you completely mad?"

"It seemed the best place. I simply asked the attendant if I might leave a carrier bag there for a time, with things that I would need someday soon. Of course she said I might. It seemed the safest place, just in case the drawing had been 'planted' on me instead of getting into my bag by mistake. I do, of course, have to consider that possibility." Phyllida uttered this Americanism without a shudder; she was concentrating on her sole. "No doubt anyone from the police to the Mafia could search my home, but it's a bit more difficult to penetrate the Lady Members' Cloakroom."

I suddenly thought of something. "Phyllida, listen: in the States, the statute of limitations on theft runs out after five years. I suppose you can be prosecuted for possession of a stolen article, but not for theft. Do you think it's worth looking into? Simply leave it in the cloakroom for five years."

Phyllida, with a touch of hauteur, ignored this.

"All right," I said, by now past amazement. "What do you want me to do? I can't penetrate the Lady Members' Cloakroom, or so I assume. Naturally, there are special facilities for guests like myself."

"Naturally, I'll get the drawing and pass it on to you. You will then return it to the museum that owns it."

"And why, when I wander in and say, pleasantly, 'You'll never guess what I found in *my* luggage,' won't they regard me with the same suspicion they would direct at you? And if your answer is that I'm not a baroness, forget it, Phyllida, it won't do."

"Do stop babbling, Anne." Phyllida was six months older than I and had always considered that additional experience of the world endlessly significant. "Here's the drill, as my father used to say. I retrieve the drawing from the cloakroom, which will almost certainly be deserted this time of night, and hand it to you in a large brown envelope I've also got in my carrier bag. You accept it happily, right in front of the man at the entrance—"

"The one with the white tie and medallion?"

"That one. I say something like 'Let me give you this now, in case I forget once we're in the taxi,' you take it, we leave the building, a nice policeman will find us a taxi, and I'll drop you at your hotel." (I always stay at a hotel in London, not being fond of joining other people's households, even Phyllida's.)

"Why are you going to pass it to me so publicly?" I asked. I know I'm supposed to be a detective and am actually rather good at it, but the thought of being handed stolen goods by Phyllida—never mind that she hadn't been the thief—was leaving me in a state typical of those who are only slowly emerging from shock.

"I'm confident you'll manage to return it to the museum, Anne; I have no doubt. I've seen you at your most inventive, as well as on the trail, and I know you'll pull this off [Phyllida liked Americanisms delivered with her best upper-class English accent] with your usual acuity. But, just in case you don't, just in case something goes, despite your most punctilious efforts, awry, we will have a witness to the fact that I handed the drawing to you and am, therefore, ultimately responsible."

I opened my mouth to protest—we were at the dessert

stage–but Phyllida held up an admonishing hand. "I've got it all worked out," she said. "Just listen. You put the envelope in the bottom of your suitcase and forget about it until you get home. Should you be, by the merest fluke, questioned by a customs person, you say you don't know what's in it, you were asked by me to deliver it to someone in New York. I've put the name of my American agent inside the envelope, just in case the worst occurs. But you will simply get home with the drawing."

She seemed to wait for me to "babble," as she unkindly put it, but I said nothing. "Coffee, my lady?" the waitress asked.

"In a few minutes, thank you," the Baroness responded, waiting until the waitress had retreated to continue outlining her preposterous plan. "After that you do this. You go to the Metropolitan Museum, look around a bit, then drift into the gift shop and buy a number of small posters–that sort of thing. Pay for them in cash. Ask for a shopping bag, though they'll probably give you one without being asked. Take it to somewhere–the cloakroom, a telephone booth, a deserted gallery–and drop the rolled-up Constable drawing into the bag. Then go to one of the places where you check your coat and packages, and check it. Walk about the museum a bit more, and then leave. End of assignment. What will happen is that eventually the unclaimed bag will be examined, the drawing found and returned to its proper owner. No doubt there will be sufficient brouhaha and much speculation, but none of it need worry you. Except–and I do emphasize, this, Anne–if anyone should recognize or greet you while you are in the Metropolitan, instantly abandon the plan."

"Suppose someone recognizes me while I'm checking the bag?"

"Then don't check it of course; wave to your acquaintance, leave the museum, bag in hand, go home, and try again, perhaps at the Museum of Modern Art."

I had to smile. Phyllida had planned it all so nicely, and I was the one taking all the risks. Except that, were I to be caught, she would step nobly in and take the blame. It had been that way at school. The plans were hers, the execution mine. We only were caught once, Phyllida immediately took the blame, and I was allowed innocently to withdraw. I trusted Phyllida. All the same I wondered, not for the first time, why I had become a paralegal and a detective while she had remained a so much more obviously conventional person.

It all worked out as Phyllida had planned it: I did my little number at the Metropolitan late one afternoon, when I thought it unlikely anyone I knew would be there. Nothing went wrong. I had brought the rolled-up Constable drawing fastened with masking tape to my blouse under my jacket. (I had suggested folding the drawing to make it small, but Phyllida had told me not to be a barbarian; Phyllida does tend to get above herself if not restrained.) After I made my purchases I dropped the drawing into the bag, wholly unobserved, in the basement, in front of some antique male statues lacking noses and penises, and indifferent to me. Then I checked the bag—excuse ready, but they asked for none—did a turn around at the Temple of Dendur, and departed.

The news of the drawing's recovery broke several weeks later. Apparently it took the Metropolitan some time to figure out what they had on their hands, and even longer to establish that what they had found was, indeed, the real thing. Endless speculation about why, who, above all where was the Vermeer. By this time I had recovered my wits and figured out, as subsequently did the newspapers, that the Vermeer had been stolen on consignment, the drawing picked up as an afterthought, unauthorized and no doubt resented. It had been cleverly dumped, as it turned out, on Phyllida.

AND THAT SHOULD have been the end of the story. The Constable drawing went back into its place at the small, elegant museum where each day it attracted a small group of viewers, and the Vermeer was, for the second time, broadly bemoaned by the media and the art world. But, as it happened, I became once again involved in this strange affair, this time closer to home and, thank God, in a more indirect way. A young art historian who had gone to work for the small, elegant museum that owned the Constable drawing and had owned the Vermeer called me up at the insistence of her lawyer husband, who knew the lawyers I worked for and had heard of my detective skills. These had become, within a small legal circle, rather celebrated. The young woman, named Lucinda, informed me that there was an intriguing and disturbing problem at the museum; she thought I might be able to advise her. When people think that problems they come across are intriguing, they are usually wrong. But I could hardly refuse to meet with her at least once, and the chance to stand right in front of the Constable drawing and admire it—which I had felt diffident about doing before—tempted me to agree to lunch and a consultation. Phyllida would, I had no doubt, have suggested a courteous refusal, but I did not consult Phyllida. We had, in fact, never again mentioned the matter of the stolen drawing, not in letters, faxes, or the transatlantic telephone conversations in which, both of us now being more than comfortably off, we frequently indulged.

. . .

LUCINDA LAUNCHED INTO her account the moment our food was served; I do like people who can come to the point. "There used to be a criminal scam going on in the museum," she said. "They found a way to stop it, and no one was fired." I lifted an interrogative eyebrow. "Oh, it was simple enough; the members of the staff selling tickets simply pocketed some of the money, not ringing up that admission. The museum blocked this scheme rather cleverly: each morning they weighed all those little buttons that would be given out when admission was paid; at the end of the day, they weighed the remaining buttons, and could therefore figure out how many had been distributed. This number had to agree with the number of recorded admissions."

"Neat," I said. "One problem solved."

"Yes." Lucinda was one of those who eat their food so slowly that I have to fight the temptation to snatch it off her plate. (At school, Phyllida used to tell me that ladies do not demonstrate quite so much enthusiasm for food.) "What has happened now is that one of the guards, who has been in the place forever, and with whom I've become friendly since we both arrive in the morning before anyone else, told me how worried he was because he was being harried by the head of security. He wouldn't say how he was being harried, I couldn't get that out of him, but he did let on that the scheme to steal the admissions money had been his— that is, Guido's, the head of security—and that Guido had taken the greater part of the proceeds, offering protection as his excuse."

"Can't you get rid of him?"

"Not easily; he's been here a long time, and is friendly with all the men on the board. They would believe him and fire the staff members. What I wanted to consult you about is that I think he was the inside man on the robbery."

"The Vermeer and all?"

"Exactly. I'd like to prove it. We could get rid of him and get the Vermeer back."

"You might get rid of him; I very much doubt you'd get the Vermeer back. I'd guess it's being held as collateral somewhere, probably in a drug deal. Your man was paid off but not, I'd guess, told who was in back of the whole thing."

"The point is, I think he took the Constable drawing when it hadn't been part of the original plan, expected to be praised, and was shocked to see it returned. If we could prove that, we'd at least get rid of him *and* get some lead on the robbery. He acted very peculiarly when it turned up here; he kept returning to stare at it, pretending curiosity, but it seemed more like astonishment to me."

"Did he say anything in particular that made you suspicious?"

"Yes; he kept asking me if I was absolutely sure it was the same Constable drawing, almost as though he couldn't believe it was. Why ask that unless he had reason to suppose it couldn't be? I think those who hired him to help in the robbery simply dumped the drawing, which they didn't want, at the Metropolitan."

"An interesting theory," I said. "Ingenious. But how on earth can you prove it was him?"

"I was hoping you'd think of something."

"Could I have the other half of your sandwich," I asked, "if you're not going to eat it?" She handed it over and we both thought and thought; I always think better while munching.

"I'll have to go away and ponder," I finally said. "But let me ask you one vital question. Please be sure of your answer. Does he suspect at all, in the slightest, that you suspect him? Would the guard, however unconsciously, have tipped him off?"

"I'm sure not: 'no' to both your questions. Guido–who by the way is no more Italian than I am, which is one-eighth–has retained his unmistakable look of satisfaction. It's because he's named Guido that we got on what he no doubt thinks of as intimate terms in the first place. He introduced himself when I first came and I mentioned that my great-grandfather was named Guido. After that we were 'chums,' even though he thinks that I, like all women, am not up to this or any job."

"You clearly can't stand the man, but apparently he's pretty widely liked. Are you sure this isn't something personal with you?"

"I hate art thieves, and people who cheat museums." And, I thought, she particularly hated this thief.

When I got back to the office, one of the partners called me in and told me how grateful the firm would be if I could help Lucinda out; something to do with her husband. "Take all the time you need, Anne."

So I began by taking the time to view the Constable drawing in place. It was still evoking comment, though it was not, I thought, that easily distinguishable from the other Constable drawings. They were all framed and under glass. When I got home I called Lucinda at her home; we had agreed not to discuss the matter on the museum phone.

"How do people go about stealing paintings and drawings?" I asked her. "Aren't they rather bulky to move?"

"With paintings, they take the canvas from the frame and then roll it up."

"Cut it out, you mean?"

"Usually. They did this time. That's why paintings on

boards are rarely stolen. With drawings, they have to deal with the glass. Drawings are always kept flat, in drawers, but when they're exhibited they're mounted under glass. Whoever stole the Constable broke the glass and grabbed the drawing; he was probably feeling confident at the time, looking for a final thrill."

"You seem to have remarkable insight into art thieves."

"Naturally; we all think about it and how it was done. That's how you prevent its being done again. There's something else I forgot to mention: the motion detectors have a record of where the thieves went in the museum. They didn't wander about. They went directly to the Vermeer and, later, to the Constable drawing. They took the tape from the surveillance cameras."

"Where were the guards at the time?"

"Tied up. They weren't involved, by the way. The whole thing's been cleared as an inside job, but of course no one ever suspected Guido. No one but me."

"Couldn't the guards give a description?"

"They did; it seems obvious the robbers were wearing wigs and false mustaches. They got the guards to open the door to them pretending to be police detectives. It's much simpler than those things are in the movies, more's the pity."

It certainly looked like a thief who knew what he was doing; of course, anyone could have cased the joint, but a visitor to the museum that attentive and that constant would have been noticed. He had led the other man right to the Constable. Had he taken a fancy to it? And if so, why? Looking around the other exhibits in the museum, I decided that one of the Constable drawings was the obvious "extra" to decide upon; why he had picked that particular one was beyond knowing, but probably he had taken the closest to hand.

Would he, given the chance, steal a Constable drawing again? Perhaps he knew their worth and had expected kudos for adding it to the Vermeer. Slapped on the wrist, he might yet, if the bait was juicy enough, steal another such drawing for his own purposes, and then we would have him. But what would be the bait? I detested the idea of entrapment, of leading someone to commit a theft he might not, on his own, have undertaken.

And then I recalled Phyllida when we were at school: she was very much the head girl–that was probably why she did so well on important boards–with me following admiringly behind. There had been a series of thefts at school, always of money which each girl kept in an obvious place. At first girls missed part of their stash (never much, gifts and allowances for food and the occasional school trip to the theater) but might have been mistaken. Then the thief got bolder and took more each time. As happens in small communities, everyone began regarding everyone else with suspicion, and as Head Girl, Phyllida knew she had to find the one guilty person to restore inno-cence to everyone else. (Now that I thought of it, that was probably the sort of thinking that had made her a baroness.) She also decided that the thief was stealing either out of need, in which case she could be helped, or out of malevolence, in which case she could be expelled. So Phyllida made it easy for someone to steal a fairly large sum of money: a girl in need could hardly resist; a malevo-lent girl could hardly resist the challenge. I tried to summon up the long-ago details: everyone learned that a stash of money was in a certain place. Not entrapment, Phyllida assured me (thought we did not, of course, use that word), because no one was being invited to steal or induced in any way. Phyllida did not take the school administrators into her confidence, and so was left (with my eager help) to deal with the results. It had a sad end, I did remember that. The girl was stealing the money for her brother, I forget why. We managed to help them out, again under Phyllida's direction.

Well, I consoled myself, what could we lose? Phyllida had asked that then, and I asked it now. Lucinda and I again met, this time not in a restaurant but in my apartment; I was not going to make finishing her food a habit. "I think we ought to offer Guido another Constable drawing," I said. Lucinda stared at me. "How does Guido regard you?" I asked. "Try to be exact, rather than modest or resentful."

"He thinks I'm in above my head, as any young woman would be. Curators should be men. He's offered to help me out, and thinks my reluctance is shame rather than distaste."

"Excellent. So if you confided in him, he would accept it as his due."

"I think so." She looked a bit wary.

"Here's what we're going to do, if you are willing. You are going to call Guido to your office in the late afternoon, one day soon to be decided upon. You are going to declare yourself in a panic. An old friend from school has pleaded with you to lend him a Constable drawing. Not that you don't trust him, but it's so irregular; no art work ever, ever leaves a museum except under the most controlled circumstances. Your friend's in a jam—don't worry, I don't think we have to explain the jam, but it's well to have a story ready. Say, your friend has to give a lecture on art theft, and wanted to make a real effect by producing a real Constable. Well, something like that," I added, as she looked more and more dubious. "Guido may well conclude your friend borrowed something and needs, temporarily, to replace it. Liars suspect everyone of lying, thieves of

thieving. Your friend's coming around for the drawing–
which you have already taken from the drawer and rolled
up–that very day. Would Guido be willing to hand it to
him when he comes by, about a half hour or so after the
museum closes?"

"You think he'll fall for that?"

"If he doesn't, we've lost nothing."

"Unless he tells people in the museum I was 'lending'
one of their Constable drawings."

"You deny it, and stick to your denial. He'll have no
proof, and he'll look foolish. He can't very well produce
the drawing if he hasn't handed it over when he should
have. You can always burst into tears at the very idea–it's
what women always do, isn't it?"

For the first time since we had met, she smiled. But she
was soon frowning again. "You're suggesting I give him a
real Constable drawing, hoping, well, expecting that he'll
steal it? What do I do after he *has* stolen it?"

"Nothing. There will be an FBI contingent there, one of
whom will pretend to be your desperate friend. If Guido
hands over the drawing, fine, we were wrong, you've got
the drawing back, no one the wiser. If he doesn't, well–
Bob's your uncle, as we used to say at school."

"I think it's risky. Why should the FBI help?"

"Stealing artifacts from a museum is a federal offense.
The FBI has been on this case from the beginning. Let me
handle that end. No one will know your part in this but
you, me, and Guido. I won't talk, and if he does, out of
honest outrage, you'll deny everything. At least you'll have
proved your suspicions wrong, and can turn your worries
elsewhere."

Lucinda agreed in the end. I was, of course, a lot more
nervous than I let on. But it all worked out exactly as I had

planned. The FBI agent, posing as Lucinda's frantic friend, turned up to be told by Guido that no drawing had been left for him. The agent withdrew, and he and his colleagues watched as Guido, the Constable in hand, departed the building some hours later; theirs was a highly effective stakeout.

Guido turned state's evidence. I don't think he knew too much about who had hired him, and they haven't yet got back the Vermeer, but everybody at Lucinda's museum is resting easier. Hopes are high.

Lucinda and her husband and the lawyers in my firm were all very happy with the outcome, and Lucinda was appointed to ask if there was anything they might offer me as a reward. I said I would like a reproduction (different size, clearly marked) of the Constable drawing that had been stolen with the Vermeer. Lucinda had one made for me, and I flew with it back to England.

I met Phyllida once again on the terrace of the House of Lords, and, as we watched the Thames and sipped our drinks, I presented her with my trophy. "You can leave it in the Lady Members' Cloakroom if you like," I said, "but I was rather hoping you'd hang it on a conspicuous wall where it will remind you of me and my talents."

"I need no such reminder," Phyllida primly said, but I knew she liked my gift. What I didn't tell her was how close I'd come to lifting a real Constable drawing. Lucinda had shown me the drawers where they were kept, and I didn't really think one would have been missed. But resisting temptation is one of the lessons I had learned at school—with Phyllida's help, of course.

AMANDA CROSS is the pseudonymous author of the popular Kate Fansler mysteries, of which *An Imperfect Spy* is the eleventh.

As Carolyn G. Heilbrun, she is the Avalon Foundation Professor in the Humanities Emerita at Columbia University. She has served as president of the Modern Language Association as well as vice president of the Author's Guild. Dr. Heilbrun's nonfiction works include *Writing a Woman's Life*, *Hamlet's Mother and Other Women*, and *The Education of a Woman: The Life of Gloria Steinem*.